FIGHTING FOR SALVATION

AUBREY ST. CLAIR

AUBREY ST. CLAIR

Copyright © 2014 Aubrey St. Clair
All rights reserved.

This is a work of fiction. Names, characters, places, dialogue, and everything else are products of the author's imagination. Any resemblance to people or events, living or dead, is purely coincidental.

ISBN: 1501067575

ISBN-13: 978-1501067570

DEDICATION

To everyone that reads and loves to escape into the fantasy worlds that writers create. It's only by doing so that those fantasies exist at all.

CONTENTS

PART ONE

Chapter One	1	Chapter Fifteen	Pg 47
Chapter Two	Pg 3	Chapter Sixteen	Pg 50
Chapter Three	Pg 6	Chapter Seventeen	Pg 55
Chapter Four	Pg 9	Chapter Eighteen	Pg 57
Chapter Five	Pg 11	Chapter Nineteen	Pg 60
Chapter Six	Pg 13	Chapter Twenty	Pg 64
Chapter Seven	Pg 17	Chapter Twenty-one	Pg 68
Chapter Eight	Pg 21	Chapter Twenty-two	Pg 71
Chapter Nine	Pg 25	Chapter Twenty-three	Pg 74
Chapter Ten	Pg 28	Chapter Twenty-four	Pg 78
Chapter Eleven	Pg 32	Chapter Twenty-five	Pg 82
Chapter Twelve	Pg 35	Chapter Twenty-six	Pg 85
Chapter Thirteen	Pg 38	Chapter Twenty-seven	Pg 90
Chapter Fourteen	Pg 43		

PART TWO

Chapter Twenty-eight	Pg 95	Chapter Forty-four	Pg 154
Chapter Twenty-nine	Pg 98	Chapter Forty-five	Pg 160
Chapter Thirty	Pg 101	Chapter Forty-six	Pg 165
Chapter Thirty-one	Pg 104	Chapter Forty-seven	Pg 172
Chapter Thirty-two	Pg 107	Chapter Forty-eight	Pg 178
Chapter Thirty-three	Pg 110	Chapter Forty-nine	Pg 182
Chapter Thirty-four	Pg 113	Chapter Fifty	Pg 184
Chapter Thirty-five	Pg 117	Chapter Fifty-one	Pg 188
Chapter Thirty-six	Pg 121	Chapter Fifty-two	Pg 193
Chapter Thirty-seven	Pg 125	Chapter Fifty-three	Pg 196
Chapter Thirty-eight	Pg 129	Chapter Fifty-four	Pg 199
Chapter Thirty-nine	Pg 132	Chapter Fifty-five	Pg 205
Chapter Forty	Pg 137	Chapter Fifty-six	Pg 208
Chapter Forty-one	Pg 142	Chapter Fifty-seven	Pg 213
Chapter Forty-two	Pg 146	Chapter Fifty-eight	Pg 217
Chapter Forty-three	Pg 150	Coming Soon	Pg 221

PART ONE

CHAPTER ONE
JOEL

"Don't get in my way, boy!" Joel's father yelled, his eyes a blaze of fury.

"Leave her alone!" the boy yelled, arms outstretched in front of his cowering mother.

The back of the man's hand moved like a flash and the boy spun as he was struck, arms flailing as he hit the ground. "I warned you. Never fucking listen to me, a day in your life. Like your bitch of a mother."

Joel's father advanced again, both hands clenched into fists of black iron, dirty from an afternoon of fixing cars and strong for the same reason. He was lurching unsteadily, so his advance was slow enough that Joel was able to scramble back to his feet and throw himself between the two adults again before his father could close the gap. His mother stood hunched against the kitchen counter, hands held protectively in front of her face.

Joel's father saw the boy moving back in front of his intended target and so he swung his right arm straight this time, trying to catch his wife before his son could get in the way. Joel grabbed the arm with his right and pushed it past his father, towards the left side of the big man's body, keeping him from using his left hand for any further striking. While he still held the arm, Joel lifted his leg and swung it into the man's exposed *belly...*

* * *

The crowd roared around Joel as his opponent stood up unsteadily after being knocked to the ground. His shirtless back was covered in sweat despite the cool breeze that blew through the alleyway, and a large gash was slowly starting to ooze blood from where he had just sliced it on the concrete. The man's right arm shot towards Joel's face, but he was too quick and he stepped out of the way, grabbing the arm with his right and pushing it left across the man's body, blocking him from throwing a punch with his other arm and exposing his belly.

With a swing of his powerful hips, Joel spun on the ball of his left foot as he brought his right leg up and out, slamming it hard into the exposed mid section. With a sharp exhalation of breath, the other man doubled over. Joel released his arm as he did and then grabbed his bent over body with both hands and pulled him forward, slamming him into the wall behind him. The man was only able to raise his hands just in the nick of time to keep himself from hitting the brick headfirst.

The crowd of 20 or so around Joel roared in cheer as arms went up and they widened around the two, shifting formation to maintain a rough circle and give them enough room to fight.

The other man, the one who just called himself "Crush", pushed himself off the wall and whirled around to glare back at Joel. He was panting now, clearly winded from the blow to the stomach, but he shrugged it off and moved forward again, bringing his arms up and squaring his hips back into his fighting stance.

CHAPTER TWO
AMBER

The only thing good about this apartment is how close it is to the subway, Amber Sinclair noted as she bounded up the stairs two at a time to emerge from the underground into the dark and cool night. She hated working the late shift at the bar, but that's where the tips were made and tips were the only salvation she had towards getting into a better neighborhood. With bars like hers, near a college, the weekends started on Thursday's.

She absently clutched her spring jacket around her. Not from the cold, since despite the breeze the night was still warm enough, but because it almost felt like it was an extra blanket of security against whoever may be lurking in the shadows. Her mother had warned her about moving into this building, but it was only at night that she really wished she had listened to her.

Her building was in sight pretty much as soon as she had come above ground, but it was still about a five minute walk to the front door. That was enough time for the creeps to settle in, so she hurried her pace. There weren't really any people around, but there did seem to be a lot of yelling coming from somewhere. As she got closer to home, the noise only got louder.

By the time she reached the front security door of her building, it sounded as if the yelling was right next to her. It took her a moment to realize that it was coming from the alleyway next to her building. Despite not really wanting to get involved, the sounds of a cheering crowd made her feel safer than she probably should feel. *You can still get raped by a group of men, it doesn't just happen with one.* She could almost hear her mother's admonishing voice in her head.

She peaked around the corner and was surprised to see a group of at least 20 in a circle, shoulder to shoulder and all yelling and clapping. They were standing too close for her to see what it was they were looking at, but she did see some females in the group which made her feel even safer. Their attention was on whatever they were watching, not her.

She inched closer to the crowd until she was standing behind one short female who she could see above. *What in the hell?*

Two men were standing bare-chested in the middle of the group, arms up defensively in front of themselves. There was a car backed into the alleyway and it's headlights were on, shining towards the group and lighting the night up.

One of the men had short cropped black hair, military style, and looked to be some sort of mulatto mix. He had a bleeding scar on his back that looked pretty fresh. He was short, and squat, but heavily muscled. One of his eyes were puffy, and his lip looked swollen as well, but the grimace on his face made it seem like those injuries just made him angry instead of hurt.

The other man couldn't look more different. He was taller, and although his body was very well defined and muscular, it seemed to be more of the kind of muscle you get from working all your life as opposed to lifting weights. He had much fairer skin, as well, and blond hair that was short but not cropped. He had an angry looking bruise on his cheekbone but other than that didn't seem to be in such bad condition.

Both men were covered in a thin film of sweat. She was about to tap the girl in front of her on the shoulder and ask her what the hell was going on when all of a sudden the shorter man charged towards the blond and grabbed him by the waist, slamming them both against the brick side of her building. The crowd around her roared and she saw a couple men high five each other. *What the fuck is this, fight club?*

CHAPTER THREE
JOEL

"Get the fuck off me Joel, or you're next, so help me!"

Joel gripped his father by the waist as his mother ran from the living room, taking the escape her son had provided for her without another thought as to what might be in store for him by offering it. He heard the bathroom door slam and the lock click. That wouldn't stop his father for long.

"You think you're big enough to stop me now, you little shit? I'll always be stronger than you. You ain't a man yet. As soon as you are, I'll be happy to kick you the fuck out of this house without having to worry about the fucking cops bringing you back."

His father pushed an elbow into the back of his neck painfully, but he held on tightly. At seventeen, he was already as tall as his father but in this position, holding him by the waist, his height was no longer an advantage.

All of a sudden his father slammed his foot down onto Joel's instep, causing him to yelp in pain and instinctively loosen his grip. His father then pried his hands off and shoved him to the ground...

* * *

Joel lifted his foot and slammed it down onto the instep of Crush, causing the man to grunt in pain and move back instinctively. His arms still gripped Joel's waist, but he could feel that the hold had loosened. Crush had stepped back enough now to let him bring his knee up and make contact with the man's groin. That caused his grip to fall away completely and Joel spun out of the hold. Crush was bent over slightly with his hands clutched between his legs, offering him no protection anywhere else.

Seizing his opportunity to put an end to the fight, Joel raised his arm and slammed his fist hard into the side of his opponents head. Crush went down in a heap immediately and the crowd surrounding Joel let out a roar.

People started to move forward now, slapping Joel on the back and congratulating him. Money began to change hands between the group, with a wad of it pressed firmly into Joel's fist. A couple of men went over to Crush and started to shake him until the man started to move on his own, and then they helped him to his feet.

"Great finish, my man!"

"Way to go. My money was on you the whole time. Fucking A."

"You ready to go again tomorrow night?"

This last question was posed by Randy, a big beefy black man who had introduced him to this group just two weeks ago after seeing him in a bar fight. Since then he had set him up with another fight almost every other night. This was the first time he had offered him another bout the very next day.

Joel nodded. "Sure."

"Great. We'll do it here again. Looks like we haven't been ratted out so we may as well use this place another night. Same time."

Joel nodded. His cheek hurt, but other than that he hadn't been injured too badly. He'd be ready to go again. A few more fights and he'd be able to afford first and last month's rent on a shitty apartment, get himself out of the shelter. He was tired of sleeping with all of his valuables up against his body under the covers. Not that he had that much to lose.

The crowd was already starting to disperse and the headlights on the car behind him shut down, leaving him in darkness as he watched the people filter away.

CHAPTER FOUR
AMBER

She couldn't believe what she had just witnessed. All of these people had been standing around watching a fight and betting on it? She was no stranger to fighting, of course, she'd seen UFC fights on TV on occasion, and although she didn't seek them out, she had to admit to getting a bit of a thrill watching two scantily clad and buff men rolling around getting all sweaty together. But in an alleyway next to her building? She would never have imagined such things actually happened.

The winner, the blond who just collected the money, still stood in the alley watching everyone else depart, as if he had nowhere of his own to hurry off to at this time of night. In the darkness, she could no longer see the sheen of sweat that covered his well defined abs, but in her mind's eye she could still imagine it. She had to admit this boy was fine, but such an animal. The look on his face as he punched the other man seemed cold, as if he didn't care at all what happened to him.

As she stared at him, only a few feet away and no longer hidden by the crowd of people, he looked up at her and caught her gaze. His eyes flickered with something, the coldness gone for a moment, and her heart started to pound in her chest as she realized that she was exposed now, and very nearly alone with a man that had just beaten someone unconscious.

His eyes seemed to pull her in as they met her own, and she could feel her heart pound even harder and her face start to flush. Quickly, she yanked her gaze away and hurried out of the alley. Fumbling with her keys, she unlocked the security door and shut it behind her, only then letting out the heaving breaths that she hadn't even realized she had been holding. She didn't even want to imagine what her mother would say to her in this situation.

She stood there for another minute until her breathing was back to normal, thinking about the tall stranger she had just watched. What did it feel like to have such power? To know that you could dominate another person so physically. She wondered if he was that dominant in the bedroom and she felt her face redden again. Shaking her head to clear such ridiculous thoughts, she headed for the elevator. It was time to get to bed. Wondering idly whether her dreams would be filled with violence and domination, she couldn't help but think that if they included the tall fighter, maybe they wouldn't be completely unwelcome.

CHAPTER FIVE
JOEL

Joel looked at his watch, a vestige of his old life and the last thing his father had given him before kicking him out of the house. It wasn't worth anything beyond timekeeping, and he wouldn't even keep the thing if he didn't need exactly that. Most people these days didn't even wear watches anymore, but he had no money for smart phones or tablets or whatever it was people used. This old Timex would do until he'd made it, and it would serve as a reminder of what he'd left behind until he did.

It was still two hours to go, plenty of time for him to get there on foot. No need to waste money on a subway when it was only three miles away from this shelter. The walk could double as a warm up for the upcoming fight.

A light rain started to fall as he walked, making the poor visibility of the nighttime darkness even worse. He didn't love the rain, although it would help cool him during the fight. The weather may also thin the crowds, unfortunately. That would affect him directly, since less people meant less money for him. Randy gave the winner 20% of the action. Last night, that worked out to almost $200. Loser got nothing but a potential hospital bill, something he definitely couldn't afford. But he'd need at least a broken bone to even consider that. He was used to pain. Pain he could deal with. Broken bones were something he couldn't fix on his own.

* * *

"He'll need at least six stitches along with the cast," the doctor said to Joel's father. "How did you say this happened, again?"

"Kids," my father said with a laugh that was almost convincing, even to Joel. It helped that his father probably did think his injury was funny. "Skateboarding accident, landed on his face and arm. We cleaned it up before we came in, got the gravel out."

"You did a remarkable job," the doctor said. Joel could see he was skeptical, but he wasn't going to get a different story out of Joel. "At any rate, we'll need to give him morphine before we set the arm. And then I'll stitch up the head." His father sat in the room the whole time, making sure Joel didn't say anything to contradict his story. On the way home, they stopped to fill his prescription for morphine pills to take for the next few days to ease the pain.

By the time they got home, his arm was throbbing again.

"My arm is hurting," he said to his father as he walked into the kitchen. His father was standing at the sink with a beer and the bottle of pills in front of him, they were already open.

His father fished a couple of fingers into the bottle and pulled out a pill. He looked at Joel and smiled cruelly, then popped it into his own mouth and swallowed it down with a swig from his bottle. "Tough luck on that," he said. "Maybe next time you stay the fuck out of the way when your mother and I are talking." He popped the top back onto the bottle and dropped them into his pocket.

Talking. That's what he called what he did with his fists.

That was the last Joel had seen of that bottle until he found it in the garbage a couple of days later, empty. By then the pain had either dulled significantly, or he had gotten use to it. Either way, he didn't care anymore. At least it hadn't happened to his good arm. He could still use it to block the old man if he had to.

CHAPTER SIX
AMBER

Another late night and Amber couldn't wait to get home and crawl into bed. She'd had a long night last night, for some reason images of the fight had kept flashing through her mind. She wasn't one for brutality, but there was just something about it that she couldn't forget. The one residual image of the tall winner staring at her as she turned away was what she remembered most. His deep eyes burned into her mind. She wondered what color they were, it had been impossible to tell in the darkness last night. In her dreams, they were golden.

Rain was pouring from the sky tonight, and she hadn't even thought to bring an umbrella. The short walk to her apartment left her drenched, and it wasn't until she was a few feet from the front door that she began to hear the familiar shouting filling her ears from the alleyway again. Her heart started to pound. Amber had assumed it would be a onetime thing, she never imagined they would be back again tonight, especially not in this weather. Despite being exhausted and really wanting to get to bed, she had to look. What if *he* was there again? Maybe if she saw him again, she could free the image from her mind and get some sleep.

The setup seemed similar with the car in the alleyway lighting the fight up with its headlights and a crowd of people circling the fighters. If anything, there were even more people here tonight and each one seemed to be cheering and yelling even louder than the other. It was amazing the cops hadn't shown up yet. In any other neighborhood they would have. In this one, they were probably too busy with more serious issues. Besides, the rain seemed to be drowning out the sound from spreading too far from the source.

Not content with looking over shoulders, Amber pushed her way to the front this time. These people were on her property, sort of, so she felt justified even though she caught a couple of dirty looks as she pushed her way through.

In the middle of the crowd, two fighters were facing each other. Their shirtless bodies were already slick with sweat and mud, obviously both men had already fallen to the ground - whether by slipping in the rain or by being thrown down by their opponent, she had no idea.

It took her a moment to recognize which of the fighters was the man from last night because of the mud. Both men were similar in size, although the new one seemed heavier, more muscular.

As she watched, the one from last night threw a swinging punch at the other man, who dodged it, only to follow it up with a kick to the thigh that made the thicker man wince and step back. Amber clapped and let out an involuntary squeal. *What the hell am I doing*, she wondered immediately. Why was she so invested in this stranger? Why should she care if he wins or loses? The only thing she should really care about was how soon it would be over, so she could head on up to bed. But her eyes betrayed her and she kept them focused on the tall man from last night.

The blond hair on his head seemed darker tonight, soaked through with rain, and his face had a stain across it that she had assumed was mud, although now that she thought about it, could just as easily be blood. How much of the fight had she had already missed?

"Who are these guys," she asked the man next to her. He was a thin man with glasses that seemed too fogged up in the warm rain to really even see anything, but she hoped he had more of an idea of what was going on than she did.

"UFC," the man said simply.

"Wait, what? The one that I see on TV all the time?" she asked. There was no way these guys were real UFC fighters, were they?

The man smiled at her. "Nah. This one stands for Underground Fight Club. These guys just wish they were in the real thing."

"Oh," she said. That made more sense.

The crowd let out a quick sound as the bigger man threw out a quick jab that caught the blond in the nose, snapping his head back. Amber sucked in a hiss and put her hand to her mouth.

"You have money on Joel? Might be a good bet, I'm taking the same gamble," the man next to her said. Joel. That was his name.

"Why?"

"He's somewhat new, but he's hungry. Haven't seen him lose a fight yet. He is a bit over-matched this time, though. Brutus is a lot more experienced."

"Why is he fighting him then?" All of sudden she felt simultaneously concerned and silly that she cared about a man she had never met.

"He was a last minute sub, although I doubt he knows that. Randy, the organizer, tells me this kid is pretty naive."

Another roar from the crowd and Amber's gaze snapped back to the action just in time to see Brutus had somehow gotten behind Joel with his arms around the smaller man's neck. Joel had one hand in between his neck and the other man's forearm, keeping him from locking the choke in completely. The two of them struggled for at least a minute and Amber was sure it was the end for Joel. All of a sudden he manoeuvred himself in such a way as to expose the other man's torso and he was able to deliver a swift elbow to the solar plexus.

Brutus stepped back and his grip loosened enough for Joel to wrench his way out, his job easier as they were both slick from the rain and mud. He pushed the big man away as both fighters paused to catch their breath, eyeing each other like wild animals.

"Whew, thought he was done for there," the man observed.

"How much did you bet?"

"I have $100 on him," the man answered.

"So everyone here just comes to watch the fight and place bets on who wins?"

"Of course," he replied, as if it was the most logical thing in the world.

"Are there rules to this... spectacle?"

"No weapons, bare hands only. Other than that, no." The man pulled his glasses off and wiped them on his shirt, as if just now noticing how wet they were. They were already splattered with fresh drops by the time he returned them to his face.

The men in the middle were circling each other again, each one looking for a weakness in the other. Amber's breath seemed caught in her throat as she watched, each nerve on edge as she waited nervously for the action to continue.

CHAPTER SEVEN
JOEL

His opponent tonight was strong, fast and wasn't falling for a lot of the tricks he'd been able to pull on fighters in the past. Joel could feel his heart thumping in his chest and if it wasn't for the pounding rain coming down and the roar of the crowd around him, he was sure he'd have been able to hear it as well. It had been a long time since he felt this emotion. Fear.

***

"Get out, get the fuck out!"
"Where the hell am I supposed to go?"
"You think I care, boy? I'm done letting you leech from me. For 18 years I've paid for everything, wiped your ass, let you eat my food. I'm done. I've been dreaming of this day."
"Fine, you fucking prick. Let me just get some stuff and you'll never hear from me again."
Joel's father laughed, but there was no joy in it. "Everything in this house is mine, boy. I paid for all of it. You're lucky I let you keep the clothes on your back."
"Are you fucking kidding me? Mom! Mom?"

"Leave your mother out of this, she's with me on this. We've both been waiting for this day. Get out before I fucking go and call the cops on you for trespassing."

A year ago, his threat would have been to kick his ass, but as Joel matured his father had begun to slowly realize that was no longer possible. The last time the two of them fought, his father had been the one that had ended up needing a doctor. No doubt that was part of why he'd been trying to get rid of him. But Joel's mother would have no one to protect her if he left. Why wasn't she sticking up for him.

"Mom?"

"I told you to get the fuck out already."

"Not until I talk to Mom," Joel said. He stood up to his full six feet two inches and pushed his chest against his father. He looked down at the older man, daring him to make a move.

"Fine," his dad said, taking a step back. "Linda, come out and say goodbye to Joel. He's finally getting the hell out of our house and leaving us in peace."

Joel's mother finally appeared in the hallway leading back to her bedroom where she'd been most of the day. A lot of times she didn't even make it out at all anymore. She was wearing a housecoat and her eyes had circles under them. From where she stood, Joel couldn't tell if they were from lack of sleep or a fist.

"Mom, I-"

"It's time you left, Joel," she said simply. She seemed to be staring at him, but when he moved slightly her eyes didn't follow. She was staring past him.

"He won't even let me take any of my stuff..." he said weakly. A pain hit him in the chest and he felt an overwhelming urge to start sobbing. He hadn't done that in years. Damn if he'd let his father see it, though.

"You heard your father," she said. "We paid for that stuff. Just get out."

"Who will protect you?"

"Fuck you, you little shit," his father said, advancing on him again but Joel pushed him out of the way and took another step towards his mother. To his horror, she took a step back, maintaining her distance.

"I got along fine before you were born," she said. *"I didn't ask for you to protect me."*

"That's right," his father sneered. *"You think you've made a difference in this life, boy? You haven't and you never will. I wish we'd never even had you. What a fucking mistake that was. God damn the number of times I think about if I had only just fucking jerked off into a tissue one more time you'd have been flushed down the toilet."*

Joel let out a scream and swung his fist, catching his father in the nose and sending him reeling back. His mother yelled and rushed forward. "Get out!" she screamed. "Just go!"

Staggering back, the young man turned and yanked open the door to his house for the last time. The night was cold and rain was coming down in sheets. His light red hoodie wouldn't protect him at all, and he had no idea where to go. His heart was pounding in his chest as he ran down the pathway leading away from his house, already drenched. What was he going to do now?

* * *

The rain pounded into Joel but his mind was somewhere else, and he didn't even notice Brutus charging at him again until it was too late. He spun to get out of the way, but the big man caught him in one of his beefy arms and pulled him along, slamming him roughly into the brick wall of the building behind him. His head snapped back and he heard and felt it crack against the stone. Immediate warmth on his neck told him it was bleeding badly.

He blinked as the air around him grew darker and it was only instinct that made him bring up his hands to protect his face an instant before he felt Brutus' fists crash into them. He could hear yelling and screaming, but all he could think about was that he hoped that it wasn't coming from him.

It's the crowd. People are watching. They're paying to watch you fight. Watch you win. Don't get paid to lose.

He shook his head to clear it even as blows continued to rain down on him. He realized suddenly he was on his knees, so he caught one of the arms of his opponent the next time he was hit and used it to yank himself back up to his feet, while at the same time pulling the big man off balance in surprise.

Joel stood up and threw a punch in the area where he thought Brutus stood, but still not seeing straight, it just went wildly past the other man and connected with nothing. The crowd around him cheered again but he had no idea what for.

All of a sudden he felt a big thick forearm wrap around his neck and slip against the wetness on his face to settle under his chin. *Fuck.*

CHAPTER EIGHT
AMBER

Amber watched in horror as Brutus held tightly around Joel's neck as the blond struggled briefly, and then went limp. The crowd was going crazy, and the man standing next to her was cursing wildly.

Brutus held on for a few more moments and then let go. She watched with wide eyes as Joel slipped out from his grasp and crumpled lifelessly down onto the pavement below. The winner raised his arms and let out a howl, almost like a wolf, and then walked into the crowd surrounding the fighters. Everyone was patting him on the back.

"Well, that's that then, time to finally get out of this rain. That's the last time I bet on the underdog," the man next to her said.

"What now," she asked. "Are they going to make sure that he's okay?"

"Who knows, who cares," the man said, turning around and starting to walk out of the alley along with many of the other spectators. "He's a loser now, no one remembers the losers."

Amber looked back at the body of Joel, still lying on the pavement. She could see that he was breathing, though, but still covered in some of the mud that the rain hadn't yet washed away. She was soaking wet as well, but barely aware of it.

No one was paying any attention to the fallen fighter, including the big black man she had seen him speaking to last night. He was too busy with his arm around Brutus, laughing and talking as if the two had just come home from watching their team win a football game.

She quickly scurried over to the fallen man and bent down, hesitantly reaching out and touching his shoulder. As she did, the lights from the car in the alley turned off and she was plunged into a heavier darkness. Joel didn't move, so she poked his soggy arm a bit harder. "Joel? Are you okay?"

Finally he started to stir. He cracked an eye open, and then another. He seemed confused and then shook his head a bit as he pulled his arms down and back underneath himself to prop up on his elbows. "What the hell..."

"You were choked unconscious," she said.

He stared dully at her for a moment, letting the words sink in until they found meaning in his addled brain. "Shit. I lost?"

She just nodded. Typical man to think about whether he won or not as he lay injured on the ground.

"Who are you?"

"No one," she said. "I mean, I was just watching... my name is Amber. Amber Sinclair."

"What the fuck do you want, Amber Sinclair," he said. He was struggling to sit up now but just as he did he swayed and put out a hand to brace himself on the ground so that he didn't fall back down. Amber instinctively reached out and grabbed him under the arm to help. He glared down at her hand.

"I'm just trying to help," she said. "You seemed to need it. No one else was going to." She looked around and noticed that they were one of the last two in the alleyway, almost everyone else had left in a hurry to get out of the rain.

"I can do just fine on my own," he said, his voice hard. He pulled his arm away from her.

"Wow, okay. Suit yourself," she said. *That's what you get for being nice in this city. Mind your business.* Her mother's voice was yapping in her ear again. She hated when it did that, especially when it was right.

She stepped back to give Joel some room. He was rude, but not really surprising given what he did with his spare time. How many fighters did she think were gentlemen, anyway?

He pushed himself to his feet and then swayed again. This time he didn't have the ground to reach out for and his arms swung wildly. Amber again instinctively reached out to help him, something she had gotten used to doing around closing time at her bar every weekend. This time Joel's hands clamped down on her arm as well as he accepted her help.

"I think you need a doctor," she said.

"Nothing's broken," he replied.

"You hit your head pretty hard. I think it's still bleeding." From the angle he was standing, she could see a trail of darkness moving down his back. She had thought it was mud at first, given the lack of light, but now she wasn't so sure.

"It'll heal."

"You really ought to get that looked at."

"I'm not paying some doctor to tell me to man up and take an advil."

"What if you need stitches?"

"Stitches are just to make a scar look pretty. It's at the back of my head under my hair. What the fuck do I care what it looks like."

"Oh," she said. She was still holding his arm and by the way he was grasping onto her, he still felt like he needed it.

"You've never had stitches, have you?" he asked.

"No."

"Well aren't you living a charmed life," he said.

"Not everyone chooses to beat the shit out of people in alleyways," she threw back.

Joel opened his mouth to reply but then shut it. He turned and looked away as the rain pelted down against his body. Amber was getting cold.

"Look," she said. "I get it, you don't want to go to the doctor. But how about I at least take a look at it? I live right here. You can come up and dry off, I can put some peroxide on the cut at least."

"Why?" he hadn't turned back to face her, he was still looking out into the night and the rain.

"Because you should at least get it cleaned and stop the bleeding."

"No, I mean why do you want to help me? What's in it for you? I haven't got any money to give you. Losers don't get paid."

"I'm not looking for money, I just want to help. Why is that so strange?"

"Nobody just wants to help. Everyone wants something," he replied. He finally turned to face her and his eyes were hard as he glared at her.

"You know what? Fuck you. I'm tired of this rain. If you want me to help clean that up, you can come. Otherwise, have a nice life." Amber turned before he could say another word and stomped off and out of the alleyway.

CHAPTER NINE
JOEL

He watched the girl, Amber, turn towards the door to her building with exaggerated footsteps, each one splashing the pavement as it stomped away. He didn't believe her for a moment that she wasn't after something, but he couldn't quite put his finger on what just yet. He clearly had nothing on him, but maybe she thought he would come back and repay her another time after being overcome with gratitude. Fat chance on that one. He could make his way back to the YMCA and his locker where he stored all of his stuff before a fight, and then find a place to sleep for the night. His head would be better in the morning.

He took one step, though, and pain shot through the back of his head making it spin again. He wasn't going to make it too far just yet. *Damn it.*

"Wait!" he called out. He wasn't sure if she heard him as she had already turned the corner and was out of sight. Could be he was too late. He walked towards the wall and put a hand on it to steady himself, following it until he turned the corner himself. Amber was standing at the door of her building, under an awning, and holding it open as she looked at him expectantly.

When he reached the door, he just nodded to her. "My name's Joel," he said.

"I know." Amber turned and walked through without another word, so he followed quietly behind her, making sure to keep a hand on each door or wall that they passed to keep the dizziness away until they got into the elevator. He leaned back against the wall of it as it started to shake and ascend.

"Don't bleed all over that," she said, looking at him critically now.

He moved forward to keep his pants and back from touching anything, but kept one hand on the wall for support.

Now that they were inside and in the light, he was able to see her clearly. Her hair was a wet mess, plastered down against her pale skin as drops of water rolled down her smooth cheeks. Her lips were puffy and full, and she had green eyes that sparkled even as she glared at him. She was beautiful, even soaking wet. He wondered again what the hell she was doing helping him.

"Where's your shirt, anyway?"

He shrugged. "In the alleyway somewhere. Probably ruined from the mud and rain at this point."

"I'm not sure what I have that would fit you," she said.

"Don't worry about it."

"Stop being an ass," she snapped. "You're injured and bleeding and I don't need a half naked man walking around my apartment." The elevator stopped as she spoke. Seventh floor.

As soon as the doors parted she stepped through and he followed as she walked down the hall to 706, fumbling with her keys for a moment and pausing before putting them in. He wondered if she was having second thoughts about helping after all.

"You're not a lunatic, are you?" she said, turning to him. "I mean, beyond willingly fighting other men in alleyways. Fuck. You are a lunatic. I don't even know your last name. What the hell am I doing?"

"You want me to leave, I'll leave," he said. He swayed a bit and then reached out to ground himself by touching the wall next to her door.

Amber looked at him, their eyes meeting for what felt like longer than was appropriate until she finally shrugged and gave a sort of half smile. She turned back to the door and put her key in, opening it. "Well, fuck it. You're here now anyway, might as well come in. You're in no shape to attack anyone now anyway, even me."

CHAPTER TEN
AMBER

The first thing she needed to do was make sure Joel didn't ruin any of her furniture by bleeding all over it, so she directed him immediately to her little bathroom, the only one in her small apartment.

"Don't mind the mess," she said. "I wasn't really expecting anyone."

Joel just grunted, his eyes looking around and taking everything in as if he'd never seen the inside of a girl's apartment before. His eyes landed on a bra she had drying over her shower rod so she grabbed it and put it behind her back. "Let me get some fresh towels, I'll be right back."

She hurried into her bedroom and shoved the bra and some other clothes she had scattered around under her bed. She shouldn't care what this man thought, and he wasn't likely to come in here anyway, but she still felt self conscious about the mess. Her mother's voice in her head was about to have a conniption.

She found some old towels in her closet that she didn't mind ruining and brought them back to the bathroom. At the door, she stood for a moment and watched the stranger she had just let into her house. Joel was studying a picture of the Eiffel tower that she had on her wall, one of the few souvenirs she had brought back from her trip to Paris the year before she had planned to start college.

He was tall. Over six feet for sure, which made him at least six inches taller than she was but it seemed like he was more than that. The muscles in his back were defined, even through the mud and blood, and the blond hair on his head could be any other color and she'd never know, given how dirty it was. But as he turned, his eyes flickered over to see her watching and they met her own for a moment before she moved in, brandishing the towels in front of her. Blue. She was finally able to see his eyes in the light, and they were deep and blue.

"Here," she said, "turn around and let me take a look."

Joel looked skeptically at her again and she rolled her eyes. Finally he turned, slowly, and presented his back to her again. She turned on the tap and put some hot water on one of the towels and then used it to wipe away some of the blood and dirt from his head and hair. He flinched slightly as she touched the wound, but didn't object.

"It doesn't look too good," she said after cleaning it enough to get a good look. The cut was deep and ran from the base of his skull up about three inches. There was a bump forming around it as well. She used the other end of the towel to start wiping away some of the rest of the dirt that covered his back.

"It's fine, I just need to rest for a couple of days. I've had worse."

"I believe it," she said softly. As the dirt came away from his back, she noticed various scars marking his upper body. There had to be at least five or six long ones and then various other smaller ones.

Joel turned, putting a hand on the towel that Amber held. The edge of his fingers grazed against hers.

"I can do the rest."

"Sure," she said. She held the towel a moment longer and then let it go. "Let me get some peroxide though. You don't want an infection. Otherwise you *will* have to go to the hospital." She opened up the medicine cabinet and pulled out a big bottle as Joel started to wipe some of the grime from his face.

He looked like he hadn't shaved in a few days, his stubble getting to a length where he'd soon have to make a decision as to whether to clear it off or just grow a beard. Even still, the hair didn't hide the strong jaw line that made up his face, or his full and positively chewable looking lips. Amber shook her head to clear that last thought. *Where the hell did that come from?*

"Turn around," she said. This time he complied immediately, still using the now dirty towel to clear off his chest. His upper body, unlike his face, was hairless but she couldn't tell if that was natural or whether he shaved it. It was covered in scars as well, but they took a back seat to the other lines that made up his midsection. Joel was very well defined, his abs looked like something out of a fitness magazine. Amber could only tear away her gaze once he had turned away from her, hiding them from view.

She took one of the clean towels and told him to lean forward over the sink. As he did, she poured the liquid onto the cut directly. He inhaled sharply. "Sorry, should have mentioned that this would sting a bit. Figured you'd be use to it."

"I am. It's fine."

The excess dripped off of him and she dabbed the cut with the towel. Fresh blood was still coming off it, so she pressed the towel firmly against his head to apply pressure. "I think you need to stop this bleeding," she said. "Hold this."

Joel reached up and around to grab the towel, placing his strong hand on top of hers before she moved it so that he could take its place. His fingers were calloused and rough, from years of working with his hands. Or fighting.

Amber stood back as she watched Joel leaning over her sink, holding the towel against his head and obscuring his view. While she had the chance, she took another long look at his hard body. Now that it was mostly clear of grime and he couldn't see her, she was able to admire the lines of his back and the sides of his stomach. He really took care of himself. She couldn't see an ounce of fat on him. His biceps were well formed and large, without being obscenely so. And his filthy pants were slightly too big, leaving them to hang low over his hips and exposing just the swell of his tight looking ass. It had been far too long since Amber had been with a man. And she'd never been with one that had a body like this. Too bad this one was so rude.

Joel stood up, still holding the towel against his head.

"You should probably keep holding that for a while. You might as well come and sit down."

CHAPTER ELEVEN
JOEL

Amber turned and exited the bathroom, leaving Joel little choice but to follow her into the small living room. He watched as she lay her last towel down on the couch. Taking the hint, he sat down on it as she dropped onto the opposite end, about two feet away from him. She was looking at him expectantly, but he wasn't sure what he was supposed to say.

"You're welcome," she finally said when the quiet grew too uncomfortable for her.

He was about to snap back at her that he hadn't asked for this, but something about the look in her eyes told him to bite his tongue. She had helped him, after all. Sure, he could have just sat down in the rain until he felt less dizzy, but she was right about an infection if the wound was really as bad as she said. He didn't need to end up in the hospital. Debt was at least one shitty thing he wasn't saddled with.

"Thanks," he mumbled. She just nodded.

"So... this fighting thing, is that a... hobby? Or...?"

Joel shrugged. "It's what I do."

"Like, do for a living you mean?"

He pulled the towel away from his head and brought it around to stare at the dark red spot that stained it. "I guess."

"Can you really make a lot of money doing that? Enough to live on?"

"I don't need much," he said. Truth was, the money started off crappy and had only recently gotten to a level where he was starting to see light at the end of his homeless tunnel. After winning a lot of fights, more people started to bet on him. But now that he'd lost...

He looked up at Amber, trying to discern the meaning behind her question. Her hair was beginning to dry and he was starting to see red coming through. Her green eyes hadn't left him for a moment as they spoke. He noted again how pretty she was, even more so now that she didn't look like a drowning rat. But the emotion he saw in her face as she looked at him wasn't familiar. What was she after? Was she fishing to see if he had money she could somehow take? Despite his initial misgivings, she didn't seem like she was after anything like that. Still, people never did anything without wanting something in return.

"Just seems like a dangerous way to spend your nights," she said. "Does your family know you do this? I can't even imagine what my mother would say..."

"They're all gone. No one to tell."

"Oh, I'm sorry."

He shrugged. In reality it was true, they were gone from his life, anyway. He found that when he said it like that, people always assumed he meant they were dead. He never corrected them.

"You live alone, then?"

"Sort of. If you consider sleeping in a room packed with strangers alone." He put the towel back against his head after finding a clean spot and then removed it. The bleeding had stopped, at least.

"Strangers?"

"I usually sleep at shelters," he said.

"Oh! I'm sorry, I didn't mean to pry."

"The money I'm making will help get me an apartment." He didn't know why he felt he needed to explain himself to her. She was nobody to him. Just another stranger with an angle he hadn't figured out yet.

She didn't say anything for a few minutes, and he was content to sit in silence.

"Listen," she said. "You're pretty covered in mud and... blood. If you want to take a shower, I can rustle up another towel. Especially if it's one you'll only use after the shower so I won't have to burn it afterwards." She laughed at her own joke but it died on her lips when she saw he didn't reciprocate.

Why was she still helping him? He still couldn't figure it out. Maybe she thought she could go through his pants when he was in the shower. She wouldn't find a nickel. "I can't pay you," he finally said.

Amber rolled her eyes again and looked at the ceiling as she let out an expressive and exaggerated sigh. "Joel, seriously, just learn to say thank you once in a while. I don't want your money, or anything else for that matter. I'm just trying to help."

His blue eyes stared at her for a moment more as he weighed his options. Finally, he nodded. "Thank you."

"Great," she said, standing up. "I think I might actually have some big sweat pants that you can wear. An old boyfriend left them here and I used to use them for bumming around the house but I was tired of always rolling up the ankles. I have an oversized hoodie, as well. Oversized for me, anyway. Still might be a bit small on you, but it's better than nothing. I'll look for them while you're in the shower. You know where the bathroom is. Just maybe be careful when you wash your head."

Amber turned and walked away towards her bedroom. Joel's eyes fell towards her ass as she did, admiring it. Her jeans were tight and well formed. She was definitely a girl that liked to keep in shape. He kept watching until she turned the corner into her bedroom.

CHAPTER TWELVE
AMBER

Digging through her closet, she finally located the sweatpants. They were a dark grey, and seemed like they would fit him around the waist for sure, but may be a bit short. Her ex hadn't been quite as tall. The hoodie she had was actually an extra large because she loved wearing oversized tops around the apartment in the winter when the landlord wouldn't turn the heat up enough, but it was an extra large woman's, which probably would also be a bit small on him. Still, she couldn't have him continue to walk around her apartment with no shirt on. It was starting to get distracting.

The pipes started to bang against the shared wall of her bedroom so she knew he'd started the shower. She grabbed another towel from her closet, one of the good ones reserved for guests. She placed the three items into a neat pile and went out to the bathroom door, intending to leave them just outside but was surprised to see that Joel hadn't closed it all the way. Maybe to allow her to drop them inside.

The mirror above the sink was in plain view through the gap, and when she looked at it she caught a glimpse of Joel just as he was stepping into the shower. The muscles on his back were rippling as he reached into the shower to pull the curtain back and test the water, but she couldn't help letting her gaze drop lower, ignoring them for a moment.

Biting her lip to hold back a gasp, she watched as his firm ass moved when he stepped over the tub and in. There was very little hair on his behind, and only a bit on his well toned legs. His back was to her, even as he pulled the shower curtain shut, leaving her oddly disappointed that she didn't get a view of the front.

Stop being a perv, she admonished herself. *It hasn't been that long!*

She pushed the door open and placed the pile she was holding on the closed toilet lid. "I'm leaving the clothes and towel here," she said.

"What?" Joel asked from behind the curtain. The running water was probably making it too loud for him to hear her clearly. Before she could repeat herself, though, the curtain was pulled to the side and Joel stood there before her, in all his glory but looking like nothing at all was out of the ordinary. "What did you say? I couldn't hear you."

"I- uh," she couldn't help it, her eyes fell immediately between his legs and her mouth opened in awe. With a mighty force of will, she tore them away from his impressive appendage and looked up at his face again. He was still looking at her with a raised eyebrow.

"Clothes," she said, pointing lamely at the toilet.

"Oh, thanks," he said. The spray from the shower was coming outside of the tub now with the curtain no longer containing it.

"You should close that," she said. She pointed at the floor.

Joel looked down and noticed the wet floor. "Oh, sorry. Right." He yanked the curtain shut.

Amber stood there, unable to move for a few more moments as his shower continued. She couldn't believe she had just seen this man completely naked. She had only just met him an hour ago! He seemed completely unconcerned as he had stood there talking to her, like he didn't even notice how inappropriate it was.

She then realized that if she was still standing in the bathroom by the time his shower was over, he was likely to end up giving her another show. The fact that she hesitated for a moment at that thought before leaving made her face get hot. She hurried out into the living room to collect herself and wait for him to emerge.

CHAPTER THIRTEEN
JOEL

The hot shower felt great against Joel's skin, as much as he hated to admit it. Certainly better than the group stalls at the YMCA where he usually took them. The water there was often lukewarm at best, and he always felt like he had to rush because there was often people waiting to get in. Consequently, showering with other people around was the norm for him, so he thought nothing of it talking to Amber with the curtain open, but he realized as soon as he saw her face that she wasn't as open.

Not his fault she had hang ups about bodies. Although he had noticed her check out his package immediately. Not that he could blame her. If the situation had been reversed, he certainly would have taken a look as well.

Just the thought of seeing Amber soaping herself up in the shower started to arouse him, and he shook his head to clear the thought. He needed to forget about that. He didn't know this girl, and he still didn't trust her. Even if she was attractive and overly friendly.

His body now clean, he tentatively reached up to touch his head to see if he'd be able to rub some shampoo through it. He winced in pain as his fingers met the cut at the back. He knew it would be even worse if he got soap in it, so opted instead to simply lean back and let the hot running water flow through his hair. It stung sharply when it hit the wound, but he ignored the pain as he watched the dirt from his hair collect along the bottom of the tub, swirly madly before disappearing down the drain. He ran his fingers through it until the water beneath him ran clean and then decided that was as good as he'd be able to do for today.

After turning off the water and pushing aside the shower curtain, he wasn't surprised to see the bathroom was empty, but he felt an odd twinge of disappointment at that fact. That feeling annoyed him slightly.

He quickly dried his body off and put on the clothes that Amber had laid out. His soiled pants were in a dirty heap on the floor, and he wasn't sure what he was going to do with them. Now that he was clean, he didn't relish putting them back on later.

"How was your shower?" Amber asked as he emerged from the bathroom. She was sitting on the couch, as she had been earlier, but had changed out of her wet clothes. She was wearing pajama pants and a white tank top. Her breasts were pressing noticeably against the fabric of her shirt and he was pretty sure she wasn't wearing a bra anymore.

"Refreshing," he said. "It's nice to be clean." He noticed her eyes again, quickly scanning his exposed chest and stomach. He hadn't bothered to do up the hoodie.

"Your head okay?"

Joel nodded, still standing by the bathroom door. He wasn't sure what to do now.

"You can sit down again," she said.

"I should get going," he said quickly. "It's late." Probably too late, in fact, for a spot at the shelter. With this rain, it was likely already a full house.

"You have somewhere to be at 1 AM?"

Amber was pretty direct, he'd give her that. And he didn't have somewhere to go, but that didn't mean he felt comfortable being in someone's debt. He was still expecting some sort of catch to all of this goodwill. On the other hand, he wasn't anxious to getting back into the rain and cold, especially with the prospect of not having a place to sleep looming.

"I thought maybe you would need to get up early tomorrow."

"No. I work in a bar, they don't even open until noon. You're welcome to stay a while."

Joel shrugged and then moved back over to the couch, across from her again. He noticed her eyes continued to stray towards his chest and abs, although she was making an effort to not make it obvious. His own eyes flickered to her chest and he noticed the outline of her nipples pressing against the cloth of her shirt.

"Does it still hurt?"

Joel shrugged. He could deal with pain.

"You do that often? The fighting?"

"Whenever they want me to. Usually every few days."

"You just fought last night as well."

"That's right. I saw you there. Randy needed a last minute replacement. I don't generally turn a fight down."

"Why not?" Amber's green eyes were wide as they spoke. He could tell she wasn't use to talking to someone like him. Her world was safe, despite the shitty neighborhood she lived in. She couldn't imagine his lifestyle.

"For the money." *Because it's all I know how to do. Because I'm alone, but pain is familiar.*

"There must be easier ways to earn money?"

"Not for me," he said sharply.

"You could get a job at a restaurant, don't discount how much you could earn in tips, or-"

"I'm not asking for career advice," he snapped.

Amber jumped slightly. He was right, she didn't have a clue about his world.

"I'm sorry," she said. "I just... it just seems so dangerous, and you got hurt pretty badly today."

Joel stared down towards the center of the couch between them. He regretted raising his voice. If she wasn't actually after something from him, she didn't deserve it after all she'd done for him. Even if he didn't ask for any of it. He never asked for anything. *Have no expectations and get no disappointments.* It was the one piece of advice from his father that he'd actually found valuable since being kicked out.

"No," he said. "It's fine. My head is okay. I've had worse. Fighting is just what I do. I've always done it. It's the only thing I'm good at. I'm not looking for anything else."

Amber just nodded slowly, her eyes on the same spot between them.

"I've watched fights on television," she said after a moment. "You seem just as good as any of them."

Joel laughed and Amber looked up in surprise. "Those guys are in a different league," he said.

"Is that what you want to do some day?"

He snorted. "I don't even dream that big."

"Why not?"

Joel threw up his hands. "How do you think you get to do that professionally? Not by fighting in alleyways. Those guys all belong to expensive gyms, they train at different clubs in different martial arts disciplines. They start off fighting in small local promotions, basically small MMA events, and then either get noticed or get a manager and try out for something bigger."

"Where do you train?"

"I don't," he said. *Not anymore.* "I was on my high school wrestling team. I did well on that. Never lost a fight. I also studied a bit of Judo and boxing after school for a few years." *If my dad had known that, he probably would have went out and took lessons himself so that he could beat me even worse. Smartest thing I ever did, doing all that behind his back.* "These days I just work out at the Y on my own."

"Clearly," she said. She was looking at his abs again. He watched her until she broke off and looked up at him. When she saw that he had caught her staring, she started to turn red.

"Umm, do you want something to eat or drink?" Amber stood up. "I need a drink." She turned and walked towards the kitchen before he even had a chance to respond.

CHAPTER FOURTEEN
AMBER

It took her a few minutes in the kitchen before she felt like her face had lost enough of its heat that she could go back in there. She couldn't believe she'd let him catch her staring at his chest. What was she, 16? He was so fit, though. She could definitely see him fighting professionally, although from what he said it wasn't that easy. Something about what he had been talking about had seemed familiar, though. She'd heard about those smaller MMA events before but she couldn't remember where.

She grabbed a couple of beers and walked back into the other room. She handed one to Joel and he took it without his usual argument. He even thanked her, which was almost as surprising as when she had heard him laugh a few minutes ago.

She sat back down and the two of them drank their beers in silence for a time. Joel wasn't much of a talker, but that didn't really bother her. She kind of just liked having a man around again. It had been a few months since she and Colin had broken up. She missed little things about his presence, like the manly smell he left on her towels and sheets whenever he spent the night. Joel finished his beer quickly and she got him another one.

"You're a bartender?" Joel asked suddenly, as he opened the new bottle.

"Currently," she sighed.

"What would you rather be doing?"

"Anything. No, that's not true. There are definitely worse jobs. It's just not where I saw myself after high school. I was going to go to college, but then I got this job and I liked having the money and freedom and the lack of homework and all of a sudden, two years later, I'm still here."

"What would you be doing then, if you had gone to college?" Joel was finally opening up and asking her questions. She wondered if guzzling the beer so quickly had loosened his lips a bit.

"I would love to be a nurse," she said.

"I can see that." His eyes flicked over to the towel sitting on the coffee table, still stained with the darkness of his blood.

"Yeah. Well, first I have to stop serving drinks for a living." She took a last sip of her beer and looked at his, it was almost empty again. "Speaking of which, do you want another one?" She couldn't believe how fast he could put them down. His belly didn't look like he was much of a drinker. Then it struck her.

"Shit," she said. "You're probably hungry, right? Do you want something to eat?" She had asked earlier but not waited for an answer, and then all she did was bring back beer. He slept at shelters for god's sake. He probably hadn't had a decent meal in who knew how long. Not to mention fighting probably worked up an appetite as well.

This time Joel seemed embarrassed. He just shrugged and looked down at his beer, his fingers turning white around the bottle as he gripped it.

"Let me see what I have." Amber went back into the kitchen and found some left over pasta she had eaten for dinner last night. She threw it into a bowl and nuked it for a minute.

"Here, have this," she said, handing the bowl and a fork to the fighter.

Joel took it with a small smile and then started to eat. The food was moving so fast into his mouth she didn't think he was even tasting it. She went back into the kitchen to get him another beer and by the time she got back out, he was finished.

"Wow, it was that good, eh?"

"Great," he said, taking the new drink from her. This time he only took a small sip before putting it down on the coffee table. "Thanks." The word was seeming to come more easily to his lips.

She didn't want to embarrass him further by asking when the last time was that he ate, but she had a feeling it had been a while. She couldn't imagine what it would be like to have to rely on handouts for everything. Especially not for someone like Joel, who seemed to hate taking anything from anyone and was suspicious every time he did. Sleeping with a bunch of strangers every night must suck.

"Listen, did you want to stay here tonight?" As soon as she said it she couldn't believe she had. Her mother's voice in her ear was silent but she was pretty sure it was because it had just fainted. "On the couch, I mean," she added.

"I don't know," he said.

"It's not a big deal either way," she said. "I just thought maybe you'd like a break from the shelter. That way you wouldn't have to go out in this rain again." Through the windows she could see that the storm hadn't let up yet. If anything, it had gotten worse. Occasional flashes of lightning lit up the room as they were talking.

She could see the indecision weighing on his face, as if deciding whether to spend the night was a life or death decision. It was almost comical to her, given that Joel was someone that punched people in the face for a living.

"Ok, sure," he said. There was another pause, because clearly manners were still foreign to him, but he finally added "thanks."

"Great. Let me get you some blankets and a pillow." She stood up, still wondering whether she was making a big mistake.

"Slater," Joel said. Amber turned to him and raised an eyebrow. "My last name. It's Slater."

She smiled, turning to head to her room to get the bedding. *Progress.*

CHAPTER FIFTEEN
JOEL

It had been more than a year since he'd stayed anywhere other than a shelter. The last time had been when he'd sprung for a hotel on his 19th birthday with some of the money he had gotten from panhandling, before he'd started to fight. He remembered how fresh and clean the sheets had smelled, and how much more relaxed he had been without having to worry about what sort of bed bugs he was laying on, or whether someone was going to try to pick his pocket in the night. He knew he might regret staying here, but in the end, the thought of another night even close to that had been too alluring.

A couch may not be better than a hotel bed, but it was miles better than a shelter cot. And he had nothing to steal with him anyway, even if he thought he had to worry about Amber. Which he didn't. He decided she was really just a sweet girl that probably would have someone take advantage of her kindness one day. People like her never stayed nice for long before they got screwed over by someone looking out for number one. Then they became bitter and jaded like everyone else.

"Joel, can you come here for a second? I could use a hand."

He bounced to his feet and made his way to the bedroom. Amber was standing on a little footstool in front of a closet with her hands above her head. The swell of her breasts caused the white shirt she was wearing to lift up, exposing her flat stomach. She wasn't as toned or defined as he was, but he appreciated that she kept in shape. Her skin was very pale, and her belly button looked like a little divot in a sheet of freshly fallen snow.

"I'm trying to get some blankets out but I have too much crap piled on top of them. Been a while since I've used these I guess." She was tugging on something that all of a sudden loosened, causing her to lose her balance on the stool and fall backwards with a shriek. Joel stepped forward quickly, snatching her from mid air in his arms.

"Oh my god," she exclaimed. Joel could feel her heart pounding in her chest even though his hands were wrapped around her back.

"You alright?" he asked.

"Yes. Sorry, I should have just taken everything off the top before trying to pull them out." She was still breathing heavily, but hadn't made a move to leave his arms. She finally seemed to realize he was still holding her when she looked up at him, their eyes meeting and their faces just inches apart. Joel could feel something as he looked down at her, but then the moment was broken as she pushed away and stood up. "Good catch, anyway." she said. "Maybe I'll let you get the pillow."

Joel walked forward and looked up to where she was pointing. At over six feet, he was able to simply reach up and grab it without issue. As he did, he leaned forward and his chest was mere inches from Amber's face. He thought she would move, but she didn't. He brought the pillow down and she still stood there, motionless.

He was close to her now, close enough to smell the rain in her still damp red hair. It was starting to curl a bit now, as it dried. He could also see freckles on her nose and the tops of her cheeks that were too numerous to count, but also so light that they almost blended in with her fair skin. Her eyes were the color of the sea and seemed just as deep.

"Got it," he said softly.

"Great," she responded, just as quietly. Her mouth was close enough to his that he felt her breath on his exposed neck. She had to look up to see his face as he stood in front of her, and he looked down. The top of her shirt was low enough that the swell of her breasts were visible from his angle, and he could see that the freckles of her face extended down onto them.

He had an overwhelming urge to kiss her just then, her full and pouty lips were parted and he could almost imagine how they would taste. It had been a long time since he'd kissed a girl. He didn't meet too many desirable women in the shelters. And unless he was missing the signs, Amber probably wouldn't object. But instead, he turned away, hugging his pillow to his hip and picking up the blankets that had fallen to the floor when she had freed them. It was late, and this wasn't a good idea. He had nothing to offer a girl like Amber. He had nothing to offer anyone.

CHAPTER SIXTEEN
AMBER

She watched as Joel walked out of her bedroom, a little wrench of frustration forming a knot in her stomach. They had been so close right there. The musky and clean smell of him had been overwhelming and she had been sure he was going to kiss her. And she would have let him. Of god, would she have let him. But then he didn't. This guy didn't make any sense.

It was probably for the best anyway. She didn't need to get mixed up with a guy like him. He didn't even have a place to live and he fought people for a living. *How much more of a Mr. Wrong can you find?* The familiar voice of her mother was back, whispering in her ear.

She followed him into the other room. He was already laying the blanket down on the couch and had removed his hoodie. The legs of the sweat pants she had lent him stopped above his ankles, they were a bit short after all. The scars on his back were white and twisted and stretched with the muscles as he set up his makeshift bed. She could imagine her hands running along those muscles, feeling their warmth and firmness. Amber blinked a few times to clear the image from her mind. *Not tonight. Not with him.*

She walked over to the couch and helped him straighten the blankets, then picked up the pillow just as he was bending down to grab it as well. Amber seized onto it first, and then Joel ended up grabbing onto her instead. His grip was strong, and his big palm completely enclosed her hand.

"Oh, sorry," she said. He turned, still hunched over, and his face was right at her level. His blue eyes were focused on her lips as she apologized. "I was-" She didn't get to continue, without warning Joel leaned forward and pressed his lips against hers. And suddenly, everything else was forgotten. The only thing Amber could focus on was Joel now. His lips pressed hard against her as his tongue rapidly invaded her mouth. She responded with a similar urgency, and pulled her hand from the pillow and his grip in order to wrap them around his muscular back and melt even closer into him.

Joel dropped his grip on the pillow as well and let it fall back down to the floor. He thrust his hands under both of Amber's arms and lifted her effortlessly off the floor, swinging her around and pressing her roughly against the wall of her living room. She reached forward to grab him again, letting her fingertips run along each ridge and muscle in his back as their tongues resumed their tangle.

She felt Joel's knee between her legs, pushing against her thighs, forcing them apart and she willingly spread them. Her hands slid down to his firm backside and she gripped it through the thin fabric of the sweat pants. His own hands ran up along the outside of her shirt and grabbed a hold of both of her breasts, squeezing and kneading them vigorously. The fabric rubbed against her nipples with each grasp of his strong hands, and she could feel a dampness start to grow between her legs.

Suddenly, she felt his hands grab tightly against the weak fabric of her shirt and pull, tearing the front of it open completely. She gasped in surprise, which made him thrust his tongue even deeper into her mouth. She closed her lips on it hungrily and tightened her thighs against his knee as well, trying to press herself more firmly against it. The roughness of his face against her skin reminded her of how masculine he was, and she breathed deeply against his face as they kissed, taking in as much of his manly scent as she could.

Joel's active hands were on her bare chest now, and he quickly grabbed a nipple with each one, giving them light tugs as they continued their urgent embrace. Little tendrils of pleasure were spreading through her chest as he continued to manipulate her nipples, and the wetness between her legs only grew hotter. Her own hands needed to feel his flesh again, so she pressed them against his back and then slid them down until they pushed past the waistband of his pants and rested against his bare ass. *God, this is the hardest ass I've ever felt.*

Joel responded by letting one of his own hands let go of her breast and drop down her body as well. He pushed past her own loose pants and dipped immediately into her underwear, pressing against her hot sex and finding the source of her wetness.

Amber threw her head back, letting it bump against the wall behind her as his fingertips penetrated her. She was pulsing with desire. Ready for him to push deeper. Ready for more than just his fingers. Grasping a hold of his muscular backside, she pulled him forward against her. She could feel the hardness of him through the pants, pressing against her stomach. She worried that he was going to be too tall, but she had no intention of letting that stop them from trying.

Sliding a hand around his hip, she didn't stop until it closed around his hot organ. It felt impossibly big as it throbbed against her palm. Joel's other hand dropped down from her chest and then he used them both to yank down her pants and panties in one pull, bending as he did so and causing her to lose her grip on his burning flesh.

His big hands clamped around her hips, his face level with her steaming sex. He was staring at her sparse red pubic hair, and she had a twinge of embarrassment as she thought back to when the last time was she had trimmed, wondering if he was disgusted by her. Almost in answer, he pushed forward and planted a kiss between her legs. An involuntary shudder ran up her spine and she opened her legs wider, but he was done there for now.

Joel's hands pulled and pushed her hips, spinning her around so that she was flat against the wall and her ass pointed back at him. She looked back at him as he stood up, dropping his pants as he did. He was enormous, and she had another thrill of fear as she contemplated what was coming and how it would feel.

Before she could think about it for too long, he was pressing against her from behind, his tip nestled against her opening which was already open and wet enough to accept him. Reaching her arm back, she grabbed a hold of his ass again and pulled him forward roughly. Joel responded by thrusting his hips up as he stood, spreading her as she was completely filled with his hardness.

Amber let out a small cry as the brunt of his impact flattened her against the wall and opened her wider than she could ever remember. She felt Joel's knees pressing against her thighs as he pushed her up, her own feet lifting from the ground with each upward plunge. She spread her legs even wider to accept him easier, inviting him to push deeper and harder with his colossal organ.

The circumstances and force of this virtual stranger made the experience hotter than she would have ever imagined, and she could feel her climax starting to build between her legs. Each slide of his hard skin along her insides made her shudder, causing wisps of pleasure to spiral up through her appendages.

Grasping her hips and moving her again, Joel pulled her from the wall and spun her sideways towards the couch until she bent at the waist, throwing her hands out to catch herself from falling and gripping the armrest. The entire time, Joel never exited her body and now that he was in a more comfortable position, his rhythm started to increase as his thighs started to slam into her behind, slapping their skin each time they made contact.

He leaned forward, snaking his hand along her skin and grabbing one of her breasts firmly again without slowing his pace. As soon as his rough fingers touched her nipple, it was enough to throw her over the edge. Amber felt her body tense up and begin to quiver. She could feel herself clamp down on the hardness inside of her, which seemed to push Joel to his own shuddering conclusion. A hot jet of pleasure erupted within her even as a loud moan escaped her lips. Every nerve ending was on fire and tingling as Joel continued to add to the wetness inside of her.

When he had finally stopped his eruptions, he pulled slowly out and this time her moan was more of a complaint at their loss of contact. He stumbled over to the couch and rolled onto it, and she followed, falling against him in a sweaty, panting heap. Neither of them said another word before falling asleep against each other.

CHAPTER SEVENTEEN
JOEL

Joel woke as the sun streamed in from the window across from the couch. He was disoriented at first, and the back of his head was throbbing along with a strange pressure on his chest. He lifted his head up and saw an arm draped across his midsection. He followed it along to see it attached to Amber, and the memory of the night before flooded back to him.

He wasn't sure what had come over him. He knew that he didn't want to get involved, and then the next moment he looked into her eyes and felt an irresistible urge to kiss her. Everything else followed from that one bad decision. Not that it felt bad at the time. It had been pretty incredible, actually. He'd never felt so raw and animalistic. It was probably one of the best orgasms of his life. But it couldn't happen again. This girl would never fit in with his lifestyle. She had a life. He had nothing. He didn't need to drag anyone else down to his level by getting involved. This was a onetime thing. It had to be.

He wasn't even sure what kind of a life he had for himself now. He'd lost a fight, he hadn't gotten paid, and he knew that losing was going to move him back down to the bottom again. Less people would bet on him, which meant he'd earn less for each fight until he could rebuild again.

But when would he even be able to do that? He reached back to touch the cut on the back of his head. He hadn't mentioned it to Amber, but it was worse than he was willing to admit. If he had unlimited money, a doctor visit probably would have been a good idea. He had no doubt it would heal in time, but he'd been dizzy on and off last night, and the simple act of sex had left it throbbing and in agony. He'd all but passed out from it afterwards. How long it would take to heal would be the biggest determining factor in when he'd be ready to fight again.

His shitty life just got shittier, and he definitely didn't need to share his misery with anyone, especially someone that seemed genuinely decent. He rarely met anyone like that in his life and he wasn't about to ruin the first one he came across.

He carefully moved her arm off of him as he slipped away and onto the floor. Amber stirred but then just turned over. She was still wearing the remnants of the shirt he had torn off of her, her back still covered but her breasts exposed. He watched as they rose and fell as she breathed. Pale mounds of flesh, crested in pink. Her chin still looked pink and raw from where his beard rubbed against her as they kissed, but her lips looked perfect. He closed his eyes, recalling how they tasted and felt against his own mouth. Then he sighed and went into the bathroom to retrieve his pants.

They were still wet, as he had left them in a heap on the floor instead of hanging them to dry. They were stiff as well, from caked on mud and grime, completely unwearable. He padded back out and put back on the sweatpants and hoodie that Amber had lent him last night. He didn't think she was going to miss them. He put back on his dirty shoes that he had kicked off by the door. Those, at least, he'd have to suffer through.

As he was about to leave, he noticed some paper and a pen by the door, so he hastily scrawled a note. With one last look at the sleeping red headed, he sighed and turned away.

CHAPTER EIGHTEEN
AMBER

"You seem in a foul mood this afternoon. Someone has their bitch on!"

Amber rolled her eyes at Simon. "I'm fine," she snapped, continuing to restock the bar with the bottles he had just delivered from the back, only this time not slamming them down quite so hard.

"Just saying girl, you need to get laid," he winked at her as he turned to return to the back room. Getting laid was always on Simon's mind, but he wasn't someone Amber ever had to worry about, unless the two of them were competing for the same man. That had happened before, and she was embarrassed that Simon had been the one to go home with him.

She wasn't angry anyway. Not really. It wasn't unexpected to wake up alone this morning, but she couldn't help but feel a bit disappointed. She wasn't really sure why. She had just met Joel, after all, and he totally wasn't the kind of guy she generally hooked up with. But still, he was raw and rough and for whatever screwed up reason, that seemed to touch something deep inside of her. The sex had been phenomenal. She'd never cum that fast from straight sex before in her life. Even if they hadn't ended up together, she wouldn't have minded having another round of that when she woke up.

Instead, she was left with only a note and a missing hoodie. That was one of her favorites, too. Warm and well worn in. The pants she could care less about, they were too big and she needed no reminders of her ex. Still, Joel probably needed the hoodie a lot more than she did. She could just get another one.

She hoisted a case of beer up onto counter and slammed it down, the bottles within it clattering together. What was she so mad about, then?

She thought back to the note she had found in front of the door. "Sorry about the clothes, I'll try to return them some time. Last night was nice."

Nice. That's what made her so mad. After everything she had done - let a stranger into her home, use her shower, wear her clothes, drink her beer, not to mention the incredible sex - and he reduced it all down to the word "nice"? She should have listened to the voice in her head and never invited him up in the first place. Or at the very least, she should have let him go after he had cleaned up. Then she wouldn't even care. She shouldn't care now. It made her even more angry that she did.

And she couldn't believe they hadn't used a condom. It didn't even cross her mind last night, she'd been on the pill forever and generally didn't use them with long term boyfriends. She wasn't use to hooking up with random strangers, but hopefully he was clean. Now she should probably go and get tested for STDs.

Simon pushed his dolly along with another load from the backroom fridge, loaded with two new kegs. "You want me to hook these up?" he asked.

Amber sighed gratefully, shooting him a smile. "Please! Thank you so much." She needed some air. "I'll make a Starbucks run, I'll bring you back a frap."

"Damn girl, you know my kryptonite. I have to watch myself around you." Simon smiled back and started to drag one of the kegs behind the bar. Amber left him and headed out in the bright afternoon sun.

It was only a ten minute walk to the coffee shop, but she took it slow. Her head was still running through the events of the previous night. Joel. "Who fights for a living, anyway?" she asked herself aloud. *Someone who has to.* The answer hit her as hard as a punch. He'd basically said as much last night, but she hadn't really understood.

She stopped in the street, making everyone else on the sidewalk have to walk around her to pass, but ignoring them. He suddenly made sense to her, the way he was withdrawn, that he lived at a shelter. Fighting was probably always part of his life. Who could guess at what sort of childhood he had, but it probably wasn't anything like hers. Fighting might be all he knew. And who was she to judge, anyway?

She slowly started to walk again. They hadn't paid him for that fight he lost, and he ended up injured, although she got the impression it looked a lot worse than it was. It wasn't like this job gave him benefits. They paid him only if he fought, and it seemed like only if he won as well. She couldn't imagine living with that sort of uncertainty and danger.

She felt bad now, having judged him so harshly. She had no idea who this guy was. For someone who fought for a living, her night could have ended up a lot worse than it did. It didn't end up badly at all, in fact. She was really just upset that it was over, not that it had ever started in the first place.

She got to Starbucks and stopped in front of the big double doors. Something caught her eye and she looked over at a large poster taped to the wall of the building next door. She'd seen it before, but never really paid it a lot of attention after reading it the first time. Now she read it over again with renewed interest. Smiling, she reached up and stuck her nail underneath the edge and carefully pulled it from the wall, rolling it up into a tube once she removed it completely. This could be helpful. But first she needed to find Joel again.

CHAPTER NINETEEN
JOEL

There was no rain tonight, but Joel was still careful to make sure he arrived at the shelter in plenty of time to get a bed. After sleeping on the couch with fresh sheets the night before, he didn't relish another night on a park bench to follow it up. Not that the shelter could compare in any way to the other activity he had partaken in last night, but going without sex again would be something he'd get use to as well.

He felt bad about leaving the way that he did. Amber had been nice to him, and really did have no expectations in return. She was gorgeous, and far more than he ever deserved. Even when he slept he didn't dream about being with women that looked like her, and never ones that treated him so well. He didn't deserve a girl like that. The best thing he could do for her in return is stay out of her life. He had no intention of going back there to see her again. Nothing good ever happened in his life, and he didn't need to drag someone like that down with him.

"Joel?"

His head snapped around and his eyes got wide. "Amber? What the hell are you doing here?"

"This is the third shelter I've been to, actually," she said. She had a small half smile on her face, but she looked at him apprehensively, as if she was expecting him to lash out at her. "I'm not a stalker, I promise."

Joel couldn't believe she was standing in front of him again. "I'm sorry I left without saying goodbye," he said. "I just thought it would be easier. Did you come for your clothes? I have them here." He turned to reach under his bunk, but she reached out and touched his shoulder.

"No, keep them," she said. "I don't care about the clothes. I just came..." she paused as he looked up at her from his cot, their eyes meeting again. He felt something between them, something he'd felt last night that had overwhelmed him enough to kiss her. He had the same feeling now, but he resisted it.

"I came to show you this," she said. She was holding out a rolled up poster so he took it and lay it down on his bed to straighten it out. His eyes scanned it quickly and then he looked back at Amber. She was smiling brightly at him.

"What do you think?" she asked. "Isn't that what you do? That sounds like a great opportunity, doesn't it?"

Joel just nodded as he re-read the advertisement. The poster was promoting a fighting competition, put on by Tiger Strike, one of the local training teams for up and coming professional MMA fighters. It was also being co-sponsored by Golden Dragon Dojos, a chain of training facilities that was known for producing some of the best fighters in the country. It was a single elimination style tournament, with spots for up to 16 fighters. First place was a thousand dollars, but more importantly, a contract to train with Tiger Strike for a full year, for free. That sort of opportunity was invaluable to someone like him.

"So are you going to do it? You should totally do it!" Amber seemed positively giddy, and he noticed that her hand was resting on his shoulder, a couple of fingers grazing lightly against his bare neck. It felt nice to be touched, his early resolve to keep her out of his life was made a lot more difficult now that she'd shown up out of the blue. And with something like this.

"Definitely," he said. Then he noticed something as he re-read the date of the fight. "Wait, this is for Sunday at 7 PM. This Sunday. As in, tomorrow."

"It is? I didn't even notice. Crap. I guess that's not going to work after all, then. I'm sorry, I should have noticed that..."

"No, this is the opportunity I've been looking for. I have to do it."

"But your head. Do you really think you should fight again so soon?"

"It's fine, it doesn't even hurt today," he lied. She was right, he definitely should not be fighting again tomorrow. Or maybe not even by next weekend. But there was no way he could pass up on an opportunity like this. Even if he didn't win, the experience alone would be worth the $100 entry fee. A minor setback towards his apartment fund, but an investment towards his future.

"Are you sure? It doesn't look so good." Amber had moved towards his back and reached out to touch the wound. He jerked away involuntarily as soon as she made contact, wincing. "Doesn't hurt at all, eh? Joel, this doesn't look better at all. I think it looks worse, actually."

"Wounds always start to look worse as they heal. You just surprised me, that's all." He turned to face her so that she couldn't try to poke it again. "Listen, thanks for bringing this to me, but you should probably go. I need to get to sleep."

"You could... I mean, if you want, you could come back to my place again tonight. It's probably more comfortable than here."

Joel looked up at Amber, wanting nothing more than to say yes and follow her back to her place. Especially if they could re-enact some of the passion from the night before. But his resolve was beginning to strengthen again. Here she was doing something amazing for him once more, giving him this opportunity that he never would have known about, and the only thing going through his mind was that the only way to repay her was to stay away.

He shook his head. "Last night was great," he said.

"But..." she said before he could.

"This isn't going to work, Amber. You know that, don't you? We're too different. I'm no good for you. The only thing I ever find is trouble, and I don't want trouble finding you."

She opened her mouth to argue but he just shook his head again. "Please," he said. "Don't come back here."

Her green eyes grew larger, and it wasn't until she turned and stormed away that he realized that was a trick of the light, shining against the tears that had started to form. He was tempted to run after her, but he gripped hard against the bed frame to hold himself back. *It's for the best*, he reminded himself. But as he lay in bed thinking about her, he was having trouble really believing it.

CHAPTER TWENTY
AMBER

Sunday was always a day off for Amber, the bar wasn't nearly as busy as people had to get up the next morning. She woke up late after a rough night of arguing with herself about whether she was more angry at Joel for being a dick, or herself for caring so much about this guy that she had known for just a day.

It had hurt more than she thought it would when he told her to leave the shelter and not come back, and she hoped that she had turned away fast enough from him so that he wouldn't see the foolish tears that started to well up in her eyes. She was happy, at least, that she held them from falling down her face. It was stupid. He was just some guy she met. Not even a successful guy. He was a fighter, for god sakes. What did she need that in her life for?

And yet, she couldn't get him out of her mind. He'd been injured, and there seemed like no one around that cared. His family was gone, all of the people who looked to be his friends the first night she saw him couldn't care less about him the next night. That would be one thing if he was a horrible person, but after spending the night with him she didn't see that side of him. What was it that kept him so alone?

He had asked her not to come back to the shelter, and she would respect that. But she knew where he was going today, at least. And she was pretty sure he wasn't going to have anyone else there to support him. He was keeping her away from some sense of twisted duty that told him he was no good for her, but that was up to her to decide, not him. She was going to the fight tonight, whether he wanted her to or not. At the very least, maybe she would stay in the back where he couldn't see her. But she wanted to see him. Make sure he was okay.

It felt like forever before it was time to leave, and even so she ended up getting there much too early so she spent some time in a coffee shop across the street, sipping a latte and watching the venue from the window. She felt almost as nervous as if she herself was going to fight. She couldn't imagine how Joel was feeling.

As soon as she started to see people starting to arrive and go in, she finished up and made her way over. She was just paying her entry fee of ten dollars when she heard some shouting coming from the back. One of the voices sounded like Joel. She hurriedly paid and followed the sounds to a black curtain at the back of the gym.

"...fucking bullshit. Fucking scam artists." It was unmistakeably Joel.

All of a sudden the curtain parted and he stormed out, walking past without even seeing her, his eyes filled with fury and likely only seeing red.

"Joel, what's wrong?" So much for her keeping a low profile at the back of the room.

Joel stopped and spun around, clearly surprised at seeing her. "What are you doing here?"

"I wanted to watch," she shrugged.

"I told you... you know what, never mind. It doesn't matter anyway, I'm not fighting."

"Why not?"

"Because this tournament is a fucking bullshit scam to drive business to this fucking club," he retorted hotly.

"Wait, slow down, what are you talking about."

"The poster said it was $100 to enter, which I brought. What it didn't say was that it was open to club members only. Fucking BS."

"So can't you join the club?" she asked. It didn't seem like that big of a deal to her. He hadn't said anything negative about Golden Dragon Dojo's last night so she couldn't imagine what he had against being a member."

"Sure, if I have $300 extra for a membership. Like I said. Fucking scam. Let's get out of here." He turned and started to walk away, not even looking to see if she followed.

"Joel, wait," she hurried to catch up to him and grabbed his arm. She knew how much this fight could mean to him.

"You don't have any other money? Isn't this worth it? I mean, I get that it's bullshit and they should have put that on the ad, but you're here now, and think about what it could mean if you win this? 300 bucks won't mean much then."

He spun around, his eyes still filled with fire. "You think I just have money lying around, Amber? Do I look like I'm fucking rolling in it over here? Everything I have I'm saving to get an apartment. To make first and last month's rent. That's a goal too. You think I want to live in a fucking shelter for the rest of my life? Yeah, if I win it I get a grand. What if I lose? There's a good chance of that happening as well. I have to fight four fucking times and win every one of them to win the whole thing. All of those today."

Amber said nothing. She didn't realize just how hard up he was. That made this opportunity even more important.

"Anyway, even if I wanted to, all I brought was $100. I left the rest with everything else I own, locked away at the Y. It starts in 20 minutes and there are no late entries. So fuck it, let's just go. Or you can stay if you want. I'm going."

He wrenched his arm away from her and started to storm away again.

"Wait," she said again. He kept walking. The club was starting to fill up now, and the noise level was rising but she knew he heard her. She raised her voice this time, though, and called out behind him. "What if I pay for your membership."

This time Joel stopped. He only stood there though, a few feet away from her, so she walked forward and around him so that she could look him in the eyes. He was looking down at her feet, though.

"I said what if I pay for your membership."

"I heard you."

"And?"

Now he did look up. His face was contorted, as if in pain. "I could never ask you to do that."

"That's fine," she said. "You aren't asking. I'm offering. You can pay me back if you win."

"Amber," he said, shaking his head. "Winning is a long shot. Let's be honest. Especially with this." He reached back and touched his head, but kept himself from wincing visibly. It still hurt, but not quite as much as yesterday.

"So, if you lose, consider it a gift. Look, I'm not saying I'm rich, if I was I wouldn't live in that shitty apartment. But on a good weekend, I can make 300 in tips alone so it's not the end of the world to me. And it's my money, I can spend it however I want. This is as worthy a cause as any."

"You just met me," he protested.

She shrugged. She'd made more impulsive decisions in her life than this one. For a lot less noble a cause.

"I don't know," he said. "I hate to feel like I'm in someone's debt."

"You won't be. Anyway, if you lose, maybe I can think of something you can do to repay me anyway." She grinned slyly and then moved closer to him. Her hand touched his stomach and then slid down his body between his legs, giving him a little squeeze. His eyes popped open and she laughed. "Just kidding," she said. "Sort of."

She let go and walked around him, heading towards the curtained area he had just come from. "Come on," she said. You only have a few minutes left to sign up."

CHAPTER TWENTY-ONE
JOEL

Joel couldn't believe what Amber had just offered him, and he really wanted to turn her down. Owing someone, anyone, something was a feeling he absolutely despised. He'd gotten this far in his life without anyone giving him anything, including his own family, so he wasn't sure how to react to it. And yet, this fight was an opportunity that could change his life. How could he turn it down?

Numbly, he followed Amber to the back where the sign ups were happening.

"Look who's back," a large Hispanic looking man said as Joel walked up to the desk. The man stood next to a couple of others that were sitting at the desk in front of clipboards. They were wearing Golden Dragon Dojo t-shirts, but didn't look like they were fighters. The man addressing Joel was wearing a white karate gi, with the Golden Dragon Dojo crest sewn onto the breast. Obviously already a member before today. He had long black hair slicked back and tied into a tight ponytail at the back. His face was worn and creased, with a small scar under one eye. One of his ears was puffy as well, clearly having been punched one too many times.

"You back to swear at our club a little bit more, ese?" the man asked, walking around the desk. He was actually about

Joel's height, but broader in his shoulders. Joel sneered at him as he approached and moved forward until the two of them were almost bumping chests.

"Maybe if your club wasn't trying to rip off fighters I wouldn't need to," he spat back.

"So maybe you should get the fuck out," the man replied, pushing forward into Joel. Joel stood his ground and didn't budge, but he clenched his fists, ready to throw down with this guy if he tried that one more time.

"Hey now, cool your jets Carlos," a voice came from behind both men. The man called Carlos glared one last time at Joel, but then stepped back. Another man was behind him, wearing a similar gi but in black. The same crest was sewn onto his breast. He had dark hair for the most part, but streaks of gray gave a hint at his age.

"Is there a problem here," he said, walking up to Joel and extending his hand. "I'm Marcus Flores, the owner of this club." Joel actually recognized his name. Flores use to be a big name fighter in MMA, holding more than one title in his day.

Before Joel had a chance to speak, Amber cut in. "No problem. We were just signing Joel up here for your event."

"Fabulous," the man said. Joel shook his hand begrudgingly, but his eyes stayed trained on Carlos behind him who was glaring right back. "Glad to have you with us. We look forward to you joining our club, regardless of how you do today. Good luck!" He gave Joel another slap on the shoulder and then nodded as he walked past him. Carlos grunted at Joel one last time and then followed Marcus through the curtain.

"Do you take credit cards?" he heard Amber say. The person at the desk nodded as Joel turned to the desk to fill out the paperwork. *I hope that fucker is fighting today*, he thought.

* * *

"You're up next," Amber was saying. "Should you head to the back now?"

They were sitting in the makeshift bleachers, a set of temporary wooden stands that were set up for people to watch the fights. So far there had been two matches out of the six scheduled for round one of the tournament. There had been only 14 entrants, which meant two fighters went immediately to round two without having to fight. Unfortunately, Joel hadn't been one of them. He had been watching the first two fights closely, but so far hadn't seen anyone too skilled that worried him. But there were still nine other fighters he hadn't seen.

"Yeah, I guess so," he said, just as he finished putting on the gloves the Dojo had lent him. He was use to bare knuckle fights in alleyways, but he'd worn these MMA style gloves before. Each fighter was supposed to be behind the curtain before their match so that they could be announced and make an entrance. Match two had just ended, which gave him five minutes before they called his name. Each first round match lasted only 10 minutes, and if there wasn't a submission or knockout in that time, the decision was made by the judges. The judges were apparently made up of MMA fighters, with Marcus being one of them.

He made his way to the back, leaving Amber in her seat. Only fighters were allowed in the back while the tournament was on. There were only a couple other guys waiting, but he knew most of the smart ones would be out watching the fights. Always made sense to know your competition.

CHAPTER TWENTY-TWO
AMBER

Amber watched nervously as Joel entered the ring. His opponent had entered first, and had gotten more cheers from the crowd than he did. Apparently he'd brought more of his own fans. Amber hadn't been the only one clapping for Joel, but she suspected most of the others had just been being polite.

The man in the ring with Joel was Sam Slaughter, and although she knew that wasn't his real name, she didn't like the connotation. Joel needed a nickname, but she knew him well enough already to know that he would think that nicknames were stupid. But still, it had to add some psychological advantage, otherwise why did everyone else seem to have them.

The bell rung, signaling the start of the match and she looked quickly at the timer on the wall. Ten minutes. He only had to make it ten minutes with this guy. He can do that. Sam didn't look nearly as big as Brutus had been. He was smaller than Joel, in fact.

As soon as it had begun, Sam rushed towards Joel trying to catch him by surprise by grabbing hold of his midsection. Joel slammed a fist against his attacker's back, but he couldn't loosen the grip. From what Amber could see, Sam seemed to be trying to squeeze the air from Joel while kicking at his legs.

With a sudden spin, Joel tripped and landed hard on his back with Sam on top. Both men scrambled around on the ground before Joel was able to fling Sam off and kick him in the chest as he tried to re-mount him. Sam flew backwards, giving Joel enough time to regain his feet.

Both men began to circle each other again. Sam once again made a sudden rush at Joel, but this time he was ready for it. Joel caught the other man as he ducked to try to take Joel down again, and he was able to wrap one arm around Sam's head. Sam's hands immediately came up to grab onto Joel's arm to try to pull it off, and she could see the smaller man struggling.

Suddenly, Joel began to slam his knee repeated into his opponent as he held him, causing the man to momentarily move his hands away to try to protect himself. She saw Joel's arm shift under the other man's neck and he began to lean back. Suddenly, Sam was slapping wildly against Joel's leg and the bell rung. The referee immediately ran between the two men and pushed Joel away.

"What happened," Amber said aloud, unsure why they were separated.

"That Joel guy just won," said a man to her left, thinking she had been asking him.

"He did? How?"

"Looked like a Guillotine choke to me. Sam tapped out."

Amber had no idea what a Guillotine choke was, but she did remember that tapping out was the equivalent of surrendering. A big smile spread across her face and she looked over at the clock. There was still over 5 minutes left on it. Joel had won very quickly.

The crowd cheered as the announcer declared Joel the winner via submission, and Amber anxiously awaited his return. When he finally emerged from the back, the next match had already begun but she wasn't paying any attention to it. She swung her arms around him immediately and gave him a squeeze. He brought his hands around her as well and she was ecstatic to feel him squeeze her back, although he pulled away pretty quickly, looking embarrassed at the public display of affection.

"You did it!" she exclaimed.

"That was only the first match," he replied. "But yeah." She was happy he allowed himself to smile back at her, even if it was very slightly.

He settled back down beside her and quickly focused on the match going on.

"That black guy favors his left too much," he said.

Amber looked at the fight in front of him, but she had no idea what Joel was talking about.

"But his opponent hasn't noticed, he keeps opening himself up to it," he continued.

She did see that one guy kept getting hit by the other guy, the black man that Joel had mentioned. She hadn't noticed before, but now that he had pointed it out, he was using his left hand more often than his right. Not something she generally would pay attention to, but apparently it was an important enough detail for Joel to notice.

The match ended with him continuing to commentate, noting each strength and weakness to her as he saw them. Most of the time she had no idea what he was talking about, but she wasn't paying a lot of attention anyway. She was mainly worrying about the next round. Before she knew it, the first round of matches were over and there were only eight fighters left.

"Ladies and gentlemen," the announcer called out. "There will be a fifteen minute intermission before we start the second round of matches."

CHAPTER TWENTY-THREE
JOEL

Joel paced in the back, waiting for his name to be called. His first match had ended quickly, but he knew that the second may not be as easy since his opponent would at least be good enough to have won his own first match. He had been lucky that Sam had been so obvious in looking for a takedown, wanting to turn the fight into a wrestling match. Normally, Joel would have no problem with that, he was very comfortable on the ground, however with Sam so interested in taking it there, Joel suspected that his standing game wasn't very strong. He tested his theory with a couple of knees to the stomach, and was rewarded when Sam flinched enough to open his neck up for a choke.

Besides, when Sam had knocked him down the first time, Joel's head had hit the mat. It hadn't hit too hard, he had made sure to tuck his chin as much as possible, but it was enough to agitate his injury. If he could avoid doing that again, he'd be happy.

The dojo wasn't posting the bracket anywhere, so he wasn't sure who he was fighting next, but he had a pretty good idea about how at least six of the eight remaining fighters fought. Two of them had moved directly to round two, so he was hoping that he wouldn't end up with one of those. It may not be a massive advantage to have watched the other guys fight just that single time, but it was something. He'd take what he could get.

He heard his name being called and he took a deep and calming breath before pushing aside the curtain and making his way to the ring. He was first this time, and he was pretty sure that he was getting more cheers than he had during match one. Clearly his quick finish had won over a few fans. But there was only one of them that mattered. He gave Amber a quick glance as he manoeuvred between the ropes. She smiled widely and he wondered yet again what he'd done to deserve her attention.

"And his opponent, from Minneapolis, Minnesota... weighing 230 lbs... Jackson Daily!"

Joel glanced towards the curtain, and the black man from the fight earlier emerged to start making his way to the ring. The southpaw.

This second match, as well as the next one, were both also ten minutes however they were being separated into two five minute rounds. That made it closer to a real MMA style match. The final fight would add a third round. He could only hope to make it that long.

Jackson was in the ring, and the referee signaled them to begin.

The two men started circling each other, each one throwing out exploratory jabs that were easily blocked by his opponent. As with his last match, Jackson was favoring his left more often. In response, Joel stepped slightly to his own left, keeping away from Jackson's power side. As he hoped, Jackson didn't compensate by moving his own stance to his right to even them up again. Now, whenever Jackson threw his left, it was a lot easier for Joel to dodge, as well as opening his opponent up in the center. On Jackson's next attack, Joel ducked to the left and then threw a right, connecting right in between the guard of Jackson and clocking him right in the nose.

The black man stumbled back in surprise and Joel followed up with a forward kick right to the midsection. Jackson doubled forward but lifted his hands in time to counter Joel's follow up hook.

Both men stood and squared off again, but Jackson still wasn't paying enough attention to Joel's stance and he was once again able to get inside the other man's guard, delivering yet another blow to his face as he stepped and slid to his left. This time, however, he also used his leg to slam back into Jackson's calf, causing the man to buckle down. He recovered quickly, though, and threw a backhanded punch toward Joel as he passed, hitting him in the back of the head.

Normally, that punch wouldn't have even fazed him, but Jackson's gloved fist had landed directly on his previous injury and an instant flash of pain seared through his brain, causing Joel to stumble forward into the ropes and allow his opponent to recover and regain his balance. As he pushed off and spun, Joel glanced up at the clock. There was still over a minute left in this round. The back of his head felt like it was on fire, and a small trickle on the back of his neck told him the cut had opened up again.

Jackson sensed that something was wrong and immediately bounded forward, swinging his left again. Joel blocked it in time, but only because he knew it was coming. He threw a jab of his own to counter, but he was slow and it was easily dodged. Jackson threw a knee forward, connecting with Joel's ribs. He sucked in breath as pain shot through him, but he was able to deflect the follow up that Jackson threw by leaning forward and into it, and then grabbing the other man and holding his arms down in a clinch while he regained his breath.

A few seconds later he pushed off, his head no longer feeling as dizzy. The clock was at 30 seconds left. Neither man was able to land anything significant before the bell rang to signal the end of the match. Joel would have 2 minutes to rest before the start of the next round.

He went over to his corner and was surprised to see Amber there.

"What are you doing here?" he asked.

"The other guy has someone in his corner," she said, with a nod of her head. He looked over and saw someone applying a cloth to the back of Jackson's neck to cool him down.

"Well, that's probably his trainer. It's not supposed to be a social break."

Amber ignored him. "How's your head. It's bleeding."

"He got a lucky hit, square in the center of it. Hurts like a bitch, but I'll be fine."

"Turn around, let me take a look."

Joel looked at her dubiously, but turned around nonetheless. He felt her press something up against it and he sucked in a breath as she pushed firmly against it.

"What are you doing back there?"

"There were towels here, I'm just applied a bit of pressure to stop the bleeding. Just hold still."

He knew it was the right thing to do, and once again he felt ashamed that Amber was constantly helping him when he could offer nothing in return. He felt her hand touch his shoulder in order to get leverage as she pushed against the back of his head. Her cool skin felt calming against his sweaty back. He almost felt himself relax, despite the situation. By the time the ref told them to wrap it up, he almost felt as if he were back at her apartment, relaxing.

The bell rang again though, and reality returned.

CHAPTER TWENTY-FOUR
AMBER

After returning to her seat, the man she had spoken to earlier looked over at her. "Are you his trainer?" he asked, his eyebrow raised. She could hear in his voice that he was pretty sure he knew that she wasn't, and so she was tempted to say yes just to see the look of surprise on his face.

"No," she finally answered.

"Ah. It didn't look like that blow by Jackson was enough to open him up like that," he said. "That was a lot of blood though."

"It didn't," she agreed. "He got that fighting the other day."

"Oh," the man said. "What club does he train at?"

"He doesn't," she said. "He fights... privately." She wasn't sure how legal what Joel did was, and didn't think it was her place to advertise what he did for a living to perfect strangers.

The man looked at her questioningly, but she ignored it and turned her attention back to Joel.

The two men were trading blows again, but it looked like Joel was back in form. Jackson had a cut over his left eye now, and was stumbling. None of his punches seemed to be connecting with Joel.

Jackson threw a swinging roundhouse which Joel ducked easily, but when the man came back around he left himself open and Joel pounced, swinging his fist upwards and connecting hard against his opponent's jaw. It happened so fast that Amber almost missed it, but she was pretty sure that Jackson's feet left the ground for a second as the punch hit him from below. He flew backwards and landed flat on his back. Joel jumped forward and landed on his chest, raising a hand in the air to continue his assault, but before he could land the first punch the ref grabbed his arm and stopped the fight. Jackson was out cold, and Joel had won again.

The crowd cheered much louder this time, but Amber wasn't sure whether it was because they were starting to root for Joel, or because the fight had ended in such a spectacular knock out. She suspected it was more of the latter, but she wanted to believe there was a little bit of both.

She leapt to her own feet and let out a holler, clapping her hands furiously. Joel's eyes scanned the crowd until they landed on her, and he gave her a big smile. Her own smile grew even wider - it was the first time he had looked that happy since she met him.

"That was a helluva KO," the man beside her said.

"I'll say," she agreed.

"Your boyfriend can certainly fight."

Boyfriend? She didn't correct him. It wasn't his business anyway, and although Joel was far from being her boyfriend, she kind of liked the sound of it.

The next match had already started before Joel joined her at their seats again. He had a new towel that he was holding against the back of his head. When he sat down, she took over holding it for him. There was ice in the middle of this one.

"That was awesome," she said to him. "You really knocked that guy on his ass."

"He was still leaving himself open," he said. "Lucky I noticed that earlier."

"It was a good observation, no luck about it," the man next to them said.

Joel just grunted noncommittally.

"How's the head?" the man asked.

Joel looked at him for a moment before saying anything. "It's fine," he said.

"Your girlfriend here said you had that going in, that guy just opened it up again. By the amount of blood that was coming out, it must have been pretty bad. I'm surprised you're still fighting with that."

Joel looked sharply at Amber, but she wasn't sure what he was angry about - the fact that she had been talking about his injury, or that he had referred to Amber as Joel's girlfriend. To her surprise, he didn't correct the man when he responded.

"Well, like I said, it's fine. This fight was today. I didn't think it was worth missing over this. Injuries happen. Part of the gig."

"It obviously isn't affecting his performance," Amber said defensively. "He's won both of his fights already."

"No doubt," the man said. He smiled and returned his attention to the ring.

After Joel shot her another look, he did the same and watched in silence. Within a few minutes, though, he began to comment on the action again. Amber took that to mean he had gotten over his annoyance.

"This guy is new, he must have been one of the Byes."

"What's that mean?" she asked.

"He didn't fight in round one because they didn't have the full 16 entrants. Big advantage for him. He's a lot fresher as this is his first fight."

Despite the advantage, however, the match ended shortly after with the fresh fighter eliminated.

Amber and Joel spoke quietly for the five minutes between rounds, waiting for the third match to start. They stopped as the announcer took his spot in the middle of the ring. The first fighter he announced was one of the ones Amber recognized from earlier. She recalled Joel saying he was quick, but seemed to lack power. He was a thin fellow with a short goatee and bald head. He had won his first round by what Joel had called an arm bar. Some type of submission.

"And next, originally from California but now a regular here at the Golden Dragon Dojo, weighing in at 245 pounds, Carlos Alvarez!" The crowd went wild as the tall Hispanic from earlier emerged from behind the curtain.

CHAPTER TWENTY-FIVE
JOEL

Joel wasn't surprised to see Carlos enter the ring, he was obviously a fighter and already a member of the club. He was actually kind of happy that he was fighting. The guy was a prick, and Joel was looking forward to being matched up against him. He wanted a chance to punch him in the face a few times.

He leaned forward in interest as the bell sounded to start the fight. The smaller fighter, Darien, seemed to run around the ring, back and forth in a confusing manner that seemed to have no real purpose. But after watching him fight the first time, Joel knew that was part of his game. Without warning, he leapt at Carlos and landed on him, wrapping his arms and legs around the bigger man after taking a running leap in an effort to throw him off balance.

Carlos stumbled, but the big man wasn't about to go down so easily. Joel saw him widen his stance and bend his knees to maintain his balance as the smaller man clung to him, and then he pulled his right arm back and slammed it into the side of Darien's ribs. The smaller man dropped off of him immediately and stumbled backwards, holding his side in obvious discomfort.

Carlos didn't waste a second. As soon as his opponent was on the ground, he pivoted on the ball of his left foot and swung his right leg around, connecting with Darien's head. The little man flew across the ring and landed on his back. He started to sit up immediately, but not quick enough. Faster than Joel would have expected for someone his size, Carlos leapt on top of him and started to pound into his head with his gloved fists. Darien started to try to defend himself, but too many blows had already slammed into him and his arms finally dropped as did his head. The ref jumped across Carlos to stop him from swinging and the match was called. He'd won in just over one minute. The crowd went crazy. Clearly Carlos had a lot of fans at the club.

Joel glanced over at Amber, and the look she gave him in return was wide eyed and full of worry. He reached over and gave her leg a little squeeze. "He's strong and fast, I'll give him that," he said. The words were out of his mouth before he realized they'd be of no comfort to her, so he hastily added "but so am I."

She just nodded, turning her head back to the ring to watch as the referee and medic sat with Darien, talking to him and making sure he was okay.

He hadn't expected Carlos to be that good. He did think he could still take him, but then again, he also thought he would win over Brutus. *I lost my focus that time. It won't happen again.*

A few minutes later, the next fight started. It went to a decision, and while the judges were talking, Joel continued to analyze the fight, correctly predicting the winner. "That's the right decision," he nodded.

They had another 15 minute break before the semi final round. Just two matches left before the finale. This time he would be fighting second.

Carlos was up first against a man who called himself Punisher. It was another two round match, but like the first time, Carlos won in the first round. It took him more than a minute, this time three of them, but it was another ground and pound knock out and the crowd roared even louder this time.

"Joel," Amber said, as he stood up to make his way to the back. "Are you sure you're okay?" Her eyes flicked down to the towel that he was holding, a dark red spot stained the center of it, but the bleeding had stopped again. For now.

"Just two more fights," he said. "Then I'll take some time before I fight again. I promise." He smiled at her, and she gave a half smile back, but her eyes were full of worry. His hand reached up and touched her cheek, running his thumb across her smooth skin. He gave it a little pat and then headed to the back to get ready.

When he got behind the curtain, Carlos was there talking to Marcus. When they saw Joel, they stopped talking and Marcus nodded at him, giving him a smile. "Great fighting, Joel," he said. "Good luck with the rest of your night." He patted him on the arm as he walked past and through the curtain to take his place back at the judges table.

"You'll need more than luck if you beat this next guy, ese," Carlos sneered.

"Why? Is your boyfriend Marcus going to fix the finale?" Joel asked in return. "That's the only way I see you winning."

Carlos took a step forward, his fists clenching.

"Bring it," Joel said, stepping toward the other man as well.

The men were toe to toe and glaring at each other as the bell sounded and the announcer started to call Joel's name. He continued to stare Carlos down and then finally stepped back. "We can settle this in the ring," he said. Carlos wasn't worth him losing his chance in this tournament. There was just too much at stake.

"Maybe once I beat you down, I'll take your little girlfriend for a spin. I bet she'd like to ride a real man. One that doesn't make her pay for his fights."

Joel paused at the curtain, his teeth clenched as he fought internally to keep from spinning and knocking some teeth loose in the fool behind him. Instead, he finally just pushed forward and made his way to the ring.

CHAPTER TWENTY-SIX
AMBER

Joel looked like he was angry when he got into the ring, which surprised Amber as he had seemed relatively calm when he had left a few minutes ago. By the time his opponent was in front of him, though, he seemed to have more of a handle on himself.

His opponent was a big man, surely out of Joel's weight class. The announcer had said he was 295 pounds and looked like he was at least 6'11. It hardly seemed like a fair fight, but she knew that the tournament was open to anyone. Even his nickname was imposing. He called himself the Steamroller.

"Nervous?" the man beside her asked.

It wasn't until he said this that she realized she was chewing on her thumbnail. She dropped her hands to her lap and gripped them tightly. "The bigger they are, the harder they fall, right?" she said.

"Something like that," he replied.

The bell rang and the men started to circle.

They started off trading blows, each man landing a few punches and kicks against the other. Within a few minutes, Joel was limping from a series of blows to the thigh that the bigger man had delivered, and Steamroller had a cut under his eye that was dripping blood down past his mouth.

Just then, Joel leapt forward with a flying punch but he was deflected as Steamroller turned away and pushed him with one big hand. As Joel landed behind him, his opponent turned and slammed his fist into the back of his head.

Joel spun around and his knees buckled. Amber jumped to her feet with a cry of anguish. That punch had looked like it was directed purposefully at his injury. "Oh my god, can he do that?" she cried out.

Her neighbor answered her. "Do what? Hit Joel in his weak spot? Of course. That's smart fighting."

That might be true, but it still seemed pretty dirty to her. Joel rolled onto his back as the big man came closer, lifting his legs to fend him off from getting on top of him.

"Your boyfriend ought to stand up if he can," the man observed. "I've seen steamroller fight before. They don't call him that just because of his standing game. He can roll over his opponents on the ground pretty good as well."

Joel was spinning on his back, keeping his legs between himself and his opponent, but each time he moved along the mat he would leave a fresh smear of blood in his wake. Finally, the ref stood him up again due to not enough action. Amber could see by the way he was swaying that he was having trouble standing, just like he'd been the other night when he'd first been hit.

She quickly glanced at the clock. He only had to last another minute before the round ended. She held her breath as she waited out the clock. Steamroller threw a series of punches, most of which were blocked by Joel but she saw at least a couple of them connect. The big man moved forward with another onslaught, catching Joel on the side of his head and dropping him to his knees again. Joel's hands fell, and Amber's heart started to pound. *Raise your hands*, she screamed in her head. *Protect yourself!*

It didn't look like Joel had anything left, but just as Steamroller was advancing, the bell ended the round and the ref jumped between them. Amber ran over to the side of the ring as

Joel slowly stood up and made his way over. His feet were still unsteady and he was blinking rapidly.

"I think you need to stop," she said when he got to her. "You're hurt!"

"I'm not giving up," he replied simply.

She picked up a towel and grabbed him by the shoulder, spinning him around and then pressed it against him again. He winced without trying to hide it at all this time, so she knew it was bad.

"Look, I know this whole thing is important, but it's not worth your health. You need to get this checked out, you might have a concussion."

"I will," he said. "I will. After I'm done tonight. I'll go in the morning. You can come, if you want." He paused for a moment and before she could say anything, he added "I mean, please come. I'd like it if you were there with me."

Amber blinked a couple of times, her eyes stinging. "Of course," she said softly.

The referee gave Joel the signal that they were about to restart and she removed the towel. The red stain was much larger than it had been last round. She was about to try one last time to stop him from continuing but the bell sounded again and he started to move away.

Fearing for what was to come, she ran back to her seat to watch the rest of the action.

"Your boyfriend should probably forfeit," the stranger said. "That wound looks pretty bad."

Amber just nodded, not wanting to take her eyes off Joel in case he needed her.

He looked steadier on his feet as he approached the center of the ring. His larger opponent wore a sneer that seemed to indicate he knew he was in the lead and expected to finish things off quickly. He started with a feint and Joel staggered to react, his earlier steadiness beginning to waver. As he moved, Steamroller followed up with a real punch that caught him in the temple, sending him reeling backward. Amber gasped as she watched him hit the ropes and use them to steady himself.

Steamroller moved forward, this time throwing a low kick that caught Joel in the shin and causing his knee to buckle slightly but he recovered and moved aside to avoid being hit by a follow up.

"Joel needs a miracle, unfortunately," the man next to her said. "Even if he makes it to the end, the decision won't even be close. If I were his trainer, I'd throw in the towel to avoid further injury. I don't think this fight is winnable."

Amber continued to ignore him. She wasn't his trainer, or manager, or anything, really. Joel would never forgive her if she made a move to try to stop the fight. But would his pride ever allow him to do it himself?

Joel was standing tall again, but limping as he circled. There was less than two minutes left on the clock and then it would be over. Amber couldn't wait for the bell to ring. She just wanted to run up there and pull him away.

Suddenly, Steamroller threw a quick jab and follow up but as Joel ducked his injured leg gave way, causing him to drop his knee to the mat. This put him underneath the guard of Steamroller, and he used that to his advantage by throwing two solid punches into his opponent's midsection.

The blows caught Steamroller by surprise and the big man doubled over in pain. Joel reached up and grabbed a hold of his head, using his neck as leverage to pull himself up and around, landing on the big man's back as he attempted to go for a choke.

Steamroller was not interested in being knocked out, though, and he stood up to his full height, lifting Joel right off the ground. He struggled to unlock the grip of the man on his back, but when he was unsuccessful Amber watched as he staggered to the middle of the ring. He bent at the knees and then threw himself backward.

She watched in horror as the two men crashed to the ground, Joel's head bouncing against the mat and then having

Steamroller's head smash into his face on the rebound. Blood sprayed from Joel's nose, but somehow his arms remained fixed under the chin of the man on top of him. If anything, the movements only served to dig him in deeper.

Steamroller continued to pry at his arms, but his strength was waning and finally the man started to slap repeatedly against his own shoulders.

The ref was on top of the men immediately, pulling on Joel until he let go. Steamroller rolled off onto his stomach, breathing heavily, but Joel just lay on the mat without moving. Amber leapt to her feet and ran to the ring, moving through the blur of tear filled eyes.

CHAPTER TWENTY-SEVEN
JOEL

He wasn't sure what had happened exactly, but it seemed to Joel as if he had woken up suddenly amidst a group of people all looking down on him with concern. He was confused at first, especially with all of the shouting and cheering going on in the background, but when his eyes finally focused he saw Amber staring down at him. As soon as she saw him open his eyes, her face split into a huge smile even as tears were rolling down her face. Joel tried to smile back, but his head felt like it had been split in two and it hurt to even move.

He closed his eyes against the pain, and was surprised again when he opened them to see different surroundings. He was lying on a gurney now, and black curtains surrounded him. Amber still stood by him, but it was quieter. There were still cheers and yelling, but they seemed more muffled and less frantic.

"What happened," he asked. His head was still aching, but it wasn't as intense as it had been.

"Thank god you're awake," she said. Tears were still filling her green eyes, but she was smiling again. He felt her hand gripping his and he squeezed it.

"The club doctor had a look at you," she continued. "He thinks you definitely have a minor concussion now, if you didn't have one before."

"I mean with the fight," he asked.

Amber rolled her eyes. "Of course. You won, you idiot."

"Really?" Joel laughed but then stopped as his head began to feel like it was going to split open from the back.

"So... the final match... I don't suppose they want to postpone it?" The look on Amber's face told him that wasn't in the cards.

She shook her head sadly. "The doctor declared you unfit to fight on, so they already declared Carlos the winner by default. I'm so sorry Joel. I know how disappointing this is."

He closed his eyes. It was the right decision of course. There was no chance he could fight on, and in the real world they didn't put fights on hold for injuries. It was just part of the job. But it burned him just the same. He felt stupid for getting his hopes up at all. A guy like him didn't get any breaks in life.

"Sure," he just said. "It's fine." The decision made sense, but he may have felt less bad about it if the winner had been anyone but Carlos. *I really wanted to get in the ring with that fuck.*

He was quiet for a little while, just holding Amber's hand and dealing with his anger and disappointment silently, like he always did. Suddenly he decided he didn't want to do that anymore. "Actually, it's not fine," he finally said, letting out a long shaky breath. "It fucking sucks." Amber was still looking down at him, and her hand tightened against his in response.

"I know," she said. Her other hand touched his forehead as she lay her palm against it. The calmness he had felt from her touch earlier returned.

"Do you think maybe... I mean, it's okay if it's not cool, but do you think I could spend the night at your place tonight? I don't really want to be alone."

The smile got even wider on her face and she ran her hand through his hair softly. "Of course," she said. "I'm so happy you want to."

"Are we free to go, then?"

"Well, I actually have to go and tell the doctor you woke up again. If you didn't, we were going to have to go to the hospital. But first, there's someone who wants to talk to you."

He raised his eyebrow at her, but she just smiled mysteriously and gave his hand another squeeze. Who the hell even knew he was here?

Amber pulled her hand away and exited the curtain. Within moments, a man walked through and up to Joel. He looked vaguely familiar, but he wasn't sure from where.

"Hi Joel," the man said. "You're one hell of a fighter," he said.

Joel shrugged. "I didn't win."

"You didn't really lose, either," the man replied. "And given the injury you started with, that's worth even more in my books."

"Who the hell are you?"

"Sorry," the man said. "My name is Shawn Rock. I run the Rock House training camp. I had the benefit of sitting next to you and your girlfriend during the tournament this evening."

That's why he looked familiar, he was the one that Amber had been talking to all night. And the name was familiar as well.

"I have to say, I was impressed by your breakdown of the other fighters from simply watching them fight, and even more impressed by how you handled yourself in the ring - especially given that you have no formal training or experience."

He would need to talk to Amber about how much she spoke about him to strangers. Where was this going, anyway?

"Thanks," he said, warily, waiting for the catch or qualifier to what he was saying.

"I recognize that you are already a member of Golden Dragon Dojo as that was a requirement of participating tonight, but I was wondering if you'd be interesting in coming to train with us instead?"

"Seriously?" Joel said, raising his eyebrows in surprise and trying to ignore that just that simple movement hurt his head even more.

"Absolutely," Shawn said. "We can't offer you $1000 in prize money, like you would have won in this tournament, but we'll happily waive all fees for joining our club and training camp. And we have an excellent doctor on staff who will take care of that head of yours."

Joel couldn't believe what he was hearing. His head was spinning, and he was pretty sure it wasn't all due to the concussion. His eyes drifted over to the curtains and he saw Amber standing by them, grinning brightly at him.

"Anyway, if you want to think about it some, that's fine. I can leave you my card-"

"Yes," Joel said. "I mean, I'll take your card as well but yes, I would definitely love to come and train with you guys."

"Excellent," Shawn said. He pulled a card from his wallet and Amber stepped forward. "Maybe I should hang on to that for now," she said.

"Please give me a call tomorrow and we'll set everything up." Shawn shook both of their hands and left the two of them alone again.

Amber walked forward towards Joel as he reached his hand out towards her. She gripped him firmly as soon as she was within reach and they both smiled at each other, no more words were necessary. He was happier than he could ever remember being, and it felt like there was a chance that maybe his life wasn't a complete waste of time after all.

He suspected this was yet another thing he would need to add to the list to thank Amber for. His level of debt to her was growing, and it seemed like it was going to take him a long time to make it up to her. Time that he'd have to spend in her company if he was ever going to even things out. But for some reason, that particular notion made him even happier. This was one debt he was actually looking forward to servicing.

Amber squeezed his hand one more time and looked down on him with her wide and beautiful smile. Her green eyes seemed to continue to sparkle even though the light in the back was dim, being absorbed by the thick black curtains surrounding them. "The doctor will be here in a minute. Once he's done, we can get out of here and head home."

Home. Joel knew that she just meant her home, not their home, but it still had a nice ring to it. He hadn't called a place home in years. "I'd like that," he replied, managing another smile of his own. He actually had a lot to smile about today, despite his injuries.

Amber bent forward until their noses touched lightly. Her breath filled his nostrils with sweetness until her lips met his gently. Their kiss was light and soft, and when she pulled away it left him wanting more.

"I'd like it very much," he said again. An unfamiliar feeling filled his chest as he looked up at this girl who had pushed her way into his life. Hope. For the first time in as long as he could remember, Joel had a feeling that the days ahead of him might actually be better than the days he'd left behind. Especially if Amber was a part of them.

PART TWO

CHAPTER TWENTY-EIGHT
JOEL

"If I had only just fucking jerked off into a tissue one more time you'd have been flushed down the toilet." Joel's dad growled, making an obscene gesture with his hands to illustrate his point. His face seemed to grow larger as he raised his fist over his head. He brought it crashing down as Joel reached up to block, closing his eyes, but he didn't feel anything.

"You think you've made a difference in this life, boy? You haven't and you never will. I wish we'd never even had you." He looked past his arms and his father was still there, his face still menacing, towering over him. He was unbelievably tall. There was no way Joel could defend against him now. He was too big. "You think you're big enough to stop me now, you little shit? I'll always be stronger than you."

"Never fucking listen to me, a day in your life. Like your bitch of a mother." His mouth grew larger, his voice roaring in Joel's ears, impossible to ignore. "You'll listen to me now though, won't you?"

"Mommy!" Joel screamed, covering his head and cowering down in the corner.

His mother appeared, her face an unreadable mask. She looked down at him and said nothing. Surely she would be on his side? He'd spent his life trying to protect her. She was his mother. She'll say something to stop him.

"Get the fuck out!" his father screamed. "We've both been waiting for this day. Get the fuck out!"

The door behind Joel flew open, wind and rain blowing against his back. And it was cold. Unbearably cold. "Mom?"

His mother looked up at him with eyes that matched the chill he felt from the darkness behind him.

"Get out." she said, staring through him blankly. She was looking into his eyes, but he could see no feelings behind them.

"But mom..." he cried now, his breathing coming in gasps. "Where will I go? Who will stop dad from hitting you?"

"I didn't ask for you to protect me!" she screamed at him. "Just go!"

Joel reached forward to try to grab his mother, hug her, beg her to reconsider - but the wind was pulling him now, like a vacuum sucking him out the door. His fingers sought to grab the door frame but they were wet with rain and he couldn't grab on. His feet lifted from the ground and he was sucked out into the darkness, his house disappearing instantly and nothing around him but the night. He screamed.

"Joel, oh my god, what's wrong?"

Joel was sitting up in bed, his mouth open and sweat covering his body. Amber had pushed up next to him and put her arms around his broad shoulders. The images were just a dream, but the scream had been real.

"Nothing," he muttered. "Just a nightmare." *If only that was all it was.*

"What about? I woke up and it sound like you were crying, and then you screamed."

"I don't remember," he lied. He'd had that dream before, or a similar one. Memories plucked out of his head and strung together to terrorize him in the night. It usually came when he was stressed or something new was happening, a change to his routine.

"Okay," she said. Amber's fingers squeezed the muscles between his shoulder and neck to relax him. "Do you think you can go back to sleep? Big day tomorrow."

"Yeah," he said, laying back down on the bed. Amber's arm still lay under his neck and she curled up to him, draping her other arm across his chest. She nuzzled her face into his neck and gave him a little kiss. Within a few minutes she was asleep again.

Joel stared at the ceiling in the darkness. It had been almost two weeks since he had even thought about his parents and his past. Things had begun to look up for him, and he was able to ignore the demons of his past while he settled in to this new relationship with Amber. But the dream was a reminder that no matter how good things got for him, his past would always be lurking in the shadows.

It was a while before unconsciousness took him again, but it continued to be devoid of peace or restfulness. The heat of the apartment didn't make matters any better, and he finally gave up trying to sleep completely when the light of dawn began to stream along the edges of their blinds.

CHAPTER TWENTY-NINE
AMBER

When Amber opened her sleep-filled eyes the next morning, a thrill of fear stabbed her as she realized the other side of the bed was empty. Her chest felt tight as she reached across the mattress, in an effort to validate what her other senses were telling her. She relaxed slightly as she grazed along the indentation that had been Joel - it was still warm, so he couldn't have left very long ago.

When a sudden banging of pipes against her bedroom started, she breathed a heavy sigh of relief. He must have just gotten up to shower. Ever since that first night when she had woken alone the next morning only to find a goodbye note calling their time together "nice", she was waiting for him to disappear again. True, it had been a couple of weeks since then, with no repeat of his vanishing act, but Joel was a hard man to read. Amber wondered, sometimes, what thoughts were behind those deep blues of his. What pain was he hiding from his past that made him so wary of any display of altruism or friendliness.

The red LED on her nightstand told her it was just past six in the morning, although the sunlight streaming in from behind her blinds seemed bright enough for noon. Joel was up early. He didn't have to be at Rock House for almost three hours. She thought he'd want to sleep in a bit more this morning to keep his energy up for his first day of training.

She slipped out from under the thin sheet that they had slept under, the weak air conditioning in her unit not strong enough to keep the warmth and humidity out of the air. A shower was a good idea. Summer mornings in this shit hole apartment always left her feeling sweaty and gross. She couldn't wait until she could afford a better place. *Until* we *can afford a better place*, she amended. She had been meaning to float the idea of Joel moving in with her. He had been staying over every night since the tournament anyway. But she knew he would balk at the idea, if only because he wouldn't be able to pay his own way. Not that she cared about that.

The door to her bedroom was closed, likely Joel's attempt to keep the noise from his shower from waking her. When she approached it, she saw herself in the mirror she had hung on its back.

Her red hair was tussled, as usual after a sweaty summer night of sleeping on it. Her green eyes were still half closed as well. She needed coffee. And both her thin white cotton sleep shirt and the powder blue panties she wore underneath were creased from the same issue that messed her hair. The top felt damp. She hated the humidity much more than the heat.

She grabbed the bottom of the fabric and pulled it up and over her head, freeing her small breasts with barely any bounce. The pale freckles from her face extended down her neck and across her chest, adding a bit of color to her alabaster skin. Her parents had named her Amber because she had come out with a full head of orange hair when she was born, but she always thought it was unfortunate that her skin was so pale in contrast. It was typical of redheads, but any time she tried to darken it by the sun she just ended up with a burn.

She left her reflection behind and walked over to the bathroom where that door was already wide open, as usual. Joel didn't seem to have any sort of privacy boundaries after years of living in shelters and showering in community stalls at the

YMCA. It was one of the more shocking things Amber had noticed about him that first night they met, but now she was use to it. In fact, it suited her purpose just this morning.

She walked in and dropped her panties on the floor, kicking them over to join Joel's boxers in the corner. She then grabbed the shower curtain and yanked it aside. Joel was just rubbing shampoo into his hair with his eyes closed, standing just outside of the stream.

"Fancy some company?" she asked with a little grin.

Joel's soapy hands paused on top of his head as he opened his eyes. He smiled as he saw her. "I feel like I'm in no position to disagree."

"Good," she said, stepping into the tub in front of him. The water behind was bouncing off of the bottom of the tub and she could feel the cool spray on her calves. "Oh good, it's not too warm." She always liked a cooler shower when it was so hot and humid in the apartment.

She looked over at the fighter's hard body, admiring his chiseled abs and well defined biceps that bulged in his current position. But the muscle between his legs interested her even more at the moment. She reached forward, taking it into her hand. It was slippery and wet, but began to stiffen in her hand giving her more to hold on to. "But it's getting warmer," she giggled.

"Let me just wash my hair out," Joel said, taking a small step back so that the spray of the shower hit his shoulders. She knew he didn't want to lower his lathered hands onto her or let the soap drip down into her face, but she liked the fact that he was sort of stuck until he cleaned it off.

She closed her hands on his flesh, pulling him gently forward again. "Leave it, I like you helpless and at my mercy." She dropped down to her knees in front of him, admiring the body that towered above her. *God this boy is beautiful.*

CHAPTER THIRTY
JOEL

When Amber surprised him by joining him in the shower, Joel had been obsessing about his restless night that had been filled with stress dreams about his past and anxious ones about his future. But as soon as she touched him, those thoughts were banished from his mind and all he could think about was the gorgeous redhead who was holding his cock and kneeling in front of him.

He inhaled sharply as she took him into her mouth, immediately rolling her tongue around his hardness and massaging his balls with her hand. He wanted to reach down and grab her head but his hands were soapy and he didn't want to get it in her eyes. Plus, she seemed to like him in this position. So instead, he gave himself over to the pleasure.

Amber continued to work on him with her mouth and hands, using her free hand now to rub along his hard shaft, following her mouth as it ran up and down its length. It felt incredible, and even though he was tired from a long night of bad dreams and little sleep, his arousal was starting to wake him up and get his blood moving again.

"Fuck that feels good," he muttered. Amber made a little sound with her mouth in agreement and continued. She let go of him with one hand now and reached around, grabbing a handful of his ass and pulling him forward into her mouth.

He took her cue and started to thrust his hips in time with her, pushing himself deeper and reveling in the increased stimulation he felt. A familiar tingling and tension began to grow in his body and he moaned a bit in response. Amber moaned as well, tightening the hand that was on his ass and pulling him even faster forward.

He couldn't resist any longer. He dropped his soapy hands to Amber's red hair and dug his fingers between the strands, wrapping them tightly to get a good grip. Guiding her head, she continued until he was ready to explode. He tried to pull her away, but she gripped onto his ass tightly until he couldn't hold on any longer. He released himself into her mouth, feeling himself spasm multiple times at the feeling of suction as her mouth swallowed and her tongue continued to stimulate his glans.

Amber didn't stop until she could tell he had nothing else to offer. Only then did she pull away and look up at him with a smile. He looked down at her with a dopey grin, and she reached up and pushed him backwards into the spray. The water fell across his lathered head, cascaded down his face and causing him to close his eyes against the bubbles.

Before he could open them, he felt Amber's lips press against his and he kissed her back, leaning forward as he knew she was probably on her tip toes to reach his lips. He wrapped his arms around her and spun her so that she was now the one under the waterfall. He pulled back and wiped away his eyes so that he could look at her.

She stood under the cool water with her head back, a smile still on her face and her eyes closed. Her small, pale breasts jutted forward, caped with small pink nipples that were like little water spouts now, directing the flow that came down from above. He reached down and kissed one of them, taking it into his mouth and giving it a soft little bite. Amber squeaked and then wrapped her hands around his head, hugging him close.

The water poured down his face as his body connected with hers, rinsing off the last of the shampoo. His mouth moved from one hard nipple to the other, and he felt Amber shiver under the touch of his tongue. His hand slipped down, starting at her flat stomach and then lower to her neatly trimmed pubic hair, and then still lower. As he touched the folds between her legs he felt her jump, letting out a little moan of encouragement.

Pressing forward, his strong fingers slipped inside of her and she gasped as she squeezed against his head. Urged on, he moved deeper into her enveloping warmth, curling his fingers and rubbing along her insides. Amber spread her legs, giving him more access than he needed for just a hand, so he took that as a hint. Joel wiggled his head to loosen her grip and then he sank to his own knees until he was low enough to face his goal. Without waiting, he pressed his lips against her tight little nub, sucking it into his mouth and then flicking it with his tongue as his fingers pushed even deeper.

Amber took a step backwards to steady herself against the wall of the shower, causing a surge of cool water to spill down across Joel's head as the shower head now directed its flow onto him. He didn't miss a beat, though. His hand moved in and out, faster now, and his mouth and tongue began to paint little invisible designs against her sensitive and engorged nerve center.

"Holy... shit..." she gasped. Amber lifted one leg, wrapping it around Joel's neck and pulling him harder against her. He responded by rubbing faster, his mouth sucking her in harder. "Fuuuuuuuccccckkkk..." she gasped, as she began to quiver and shake. Her leg squeezed around his neck like she was putting him in a triangle choke, but he held on as his fingers and tongue continued their assault. Finally, she had had enough and loosed her grip, pushing his head away.

The water poured forth against face until Amber moved forward, cutting off the flow from reaching him. She put a hand on his arm and yanked until he stood up, pulling him in for a deep kiss.

CHAPTER THIRTY-ONE
AMBER

Joel left the shower first, since he was just finishing up when Amber had arrived. She watched his tight wet ass step over the tub as he disappeared behind the shower curtain and bit her lip. The pleasure from her orgasm a few minutes ago had still not completely dissipated, and just the sight of his hard body made her feel tingly all over again. She wondered whether or not she could entice him into bending her over the bed and taking her hard before he had to get ready to leave.

The mental image of Joel behind her with his powerful hands on her hips, filling her as their bodies were pulled together made her face feel hot, so she turned the knob to reduce the water temperature even more. If she was going to try to have sex with Joel, she wanted to cool down completely before venturing back out into the warm apartment - otherwise the heat from their bodies would make it even more uncomfortable.

She quickly finished her shower and stepped out, toweling off quickly before leaving the bathroom, still naked, in search of Joel.

She found him in the bedroom, already half dressed.

"Hey," he said, nodding at her. She noted his eyes roam over her body as a little smile formed on his chewable lips.

"Hey yourself, stud," she said with a little wink. She walked forward and slid a hand into his still open jeans, grabbing him firmly. He was soft now, but she knew she could fix that soon enough.

Joel chuckled and then stepped back, causing her hand to fall out of his pants. "Not now," he said. I have to get ready and get going.

She frowned at him and quickly glanced at the clock. "It's not even seven. I thought you don't have to be there until nine?"

Joel zipped up his pants and fastened them, as if to lock himself away in case she tried to grab him again. "I do, but I have to stop by the Y and get a couple things from my locker. And I want to get there early, anyway. First day and all."

Amber's frown deepened. She picked up her comfy pajama pants and slipped them on now that she knew Joel wasn't interested. "Why do you even still have a locker there?" she asked.

"What do you mean? I need a place to store my stuff."

"You can leave it here. Anyway, I was thinking that maybe you should just move in. Like, officially."

Joel paused in the middle of pulling on a light short sleeved shirt, his head about to disappear underneath the cotton. He gave her a weird look and then pulled it on. By the time his head had emerged again, his face had darkened a bit.

"Amber, I thought you understood, I don't have money to pay for a place. After I paid you back for the tournament, and the fact that I haven't fought in a couple of weeks, my savings-"

"I told you that entry fee was a gift, I didn't want you to pay me back unless you won."

"And I told you I don't like being in debt to people."

"Whatever. Look, I'm not asking you to pay for rent. I'm just saying that you might as well move in-"

"Which would put me right back into debt to you!" he said, his voice raising in frustration.

"So what? What's the difference anyway? You've been here every night since the tournament and you're not paying me now."

His eyes flashed in anger. "You're right. You're absolutely right. I should pay you for the time I've spent here."

"That's not what I'm saying," she said, shaking her head. He could be such a hot head, especially around money and debt. It frustrated her.

"No, that's what I'm saying. I've been freeloading and it's time it stopped. That's one lesson I learned from Darryl and Linda, at least. *There ain't nothing in this life that's yours that you haven't paid for.* I'll go back to the shelter tonight after training." Amber always thought it was sad that he referred to his parents by their first names on the rare occasion that he brought them up. Fully dressed now, Joel pushed past her and left the bedroom. Amber grabbed her own shirt and pulled it on as she followed after him.

"Joel, don't be an idiot."

He stood by the door, pulling on his shoes and not looking up at her. She could see he was fuming.

"This is silly. I don't want your money, I just want you. I can pay for the rent. I've been doing that since I started living on my own."

"Well congratulations on being so together with your life," he spat. "Not everyone got such a positive head start in life." He stood up and spun around without looking at her, yanking the door open.

"Joel, wait! Don't leave like this. Come back after training and let's talk."

"I have nothing more to say." With that he stepped out into the hallway and pulled the door shut behind him with a bang.

Amber let out a shuddering breath, her eyes starting to sting a bit. *What the fuck was that all about?*

CHAPTER THIRTY-TWO
JOEL

Joel stomped through the city towards the YMCA, his shirt already wet with sweat. He had originally planned on taking a bus, but after the fight with Amber he decided to walk off his frustrations. He had plenty of time before he needed to be at Rock House anyway.

He kicked a loose piece of concrete hard, sending it skittering into the road. An oncoming car swerved to miss it and honked at him angrily. He threw up his middle finger and kept walking. The one feeling he hated more than any other was that he owed someone something. His parents had kicked him out with only the clothes on his back, and from then on he learned to rely only on himself. *If you rely on other people for things, you're in for disappointment.*

He owed Amber more than anyone. She was the one that helped him that night he was injured. She was the one that found the tournament and sought him out to convince him to try it. She was the one that paid for his membership - although at least he had been able to pay her back for that. There wasn't a lot he could do about the others; it was harder to pay back gestures.

But she was right. He was basically living with her rent free, which was just racking up his debt to her. The fact that they were... what? Seeing each other? Boyfriend and girlfriend? They had never defined it - but anyway, it didn't matter. It was still freeloading and it had to stop. Unfortunately, he was just about broke. Paying her back the $300 to join Golden Dragon had taken most of his savings, and he had used the rest to buy some of the training equipment that Shawn had told him he would need before starting at Rock House.

The equipment was what he needed from his locker. He hadn't brought it back to the apartment because he didn't want Amber to ask questions about it. He knew she would offer to pay for them or something, which would have just ended them up in the same fight they just had. The whole argument was unavoidable, with no money it was bound to come up sometime.

He could see the YMCA in the distance now, it would only be another 20 minutes or so before he got there. He considered having another quick shower to clean off the sweat and then change into another shirt, but there was no point. He'd just get sweaty again once he started training.

Was this relationship with Amber really going to work? They were so different. She may live in a crappy apartment, but at least it was a stable roof over her head and her own bed at night. And at the end of the day, if things went bad she could always go back home to her parents. She had a safety net, and she couldn't comprehend what life was like without one.

And yet, he wanted things to work. Even though deep down he knew he didn't deserve someone like Amber, not by a long shot, he still wanted her. She was kind hearted. More so than anyone he'd ever met. And when she turned that kindness towards him, it made the bleakness of his existence just a little bit brighter.

It didn't hurt that she also gorgeous. Especially naked. A smile crept across his face as he pictured her. It had been a long time since a girl had offered herself to him the way Amber did - exposed and vulnerable. Even in bed she was giving, always putting his pleasure above her own.

It made him feel guilty sometimes, adding to an internal debt tally that just grew and grew with no hope that he could ever repay it. Adding money to that list as well, something he *could* repay if he was more successful, just made him feel even worse. Maybe if life had given him a few more breaks instead of just constantly finding new ways to remind him of his failures.

That was what had made him so angry at the apartment. He hadn't even considered the fact that he was freeloading, living with her this past week while she continued to pay the rent, the bills, even buy all the food. She may not have been accusing him of it, but bringing it up made him realize he was just digging himself in deeper with her, and he really had no plan to even things out.

Shawn Rock had offered to train him, but that wasn't going to earn Joel any money. And even if he could find a job, there was no time for it now since he'd be training during the days and needing his sleep at night. There was only one thing he was qualified to do anyway. Joel squeezed his fists.

He'd promised Amber that now that he was going to train at Rock House he would give up fighting at nights. But if he did, he'd have no money at all. Yet he really did want to live with her - he just wasn't willing to do it for free. He needed to pay his own way. If he couldn't, then he didn't see a lot of hope for a future between them.

Surely breaking that promise was better than breaking their relationship. That rationalization solidified the decision in his mind, although he knew he had to keep it to himself, at least for now.

First thing he had to do was track down Randy, the organizer of the underground fight club. He had an idea of how to do that, but it would have to wait until after today's training session.

CHAPTER THIRTY-THREE
AMBER

Amber spent most of the rest of the morning angry and confused. How did a morning that started off with a sexy shower end up in a fight like that? It had all happened so fast, she was confused about what exactly it was even about. Joel was quick to anger, she knew that about him, but she thought they had been getting to a good place and he was really starting to trust her. Now he was painting her as a gold digger looking to dip her hands into his pockets. That wasn't what she meant at all.

She had been paying rent on this place on her own for almost two years, she didn't need him to chip in. Sure, it would help in the sense that then she could save for an even better place, with him, but that wasn't even her goal. It had really just been an innocent suggestion. Why did he fly off the handle like that?

What burned her the most was his comment about her "head start". She bit her lip in frustration. What did he know about her home life, anyway? He never once asked about it, and she knew better than to dare and ask about his. Her parents didn't give her anything to help with this place, if that's what he meant. They hated that she lived here, but it wasn't like they ever offered to help her find anything else. They lived in their own little bubble, making comments about everyone else's life and affairs without ever lifting a finger to change anything. Full of advice and no action.

Still, Amber had a feeling she did know what Joel was talking about. She had suspicions that Joel's home life was pretty bad. One didn't end up living in shelters and fighting for a living after growing up in a happy and positive environment. She couldn't imagine what it must have been like, but she hoped one day he would open up and tell her. For now she would leave it alone. He had mentioned once that the shitty apartment she lived in was at least in a better neighborhood than where he came from. When he told her where that was, she had to agree - he grew up in the worst part of town.

But other than a rough idea of where he had grown up, the only other thing she ever really got out of him was that his parents were gone now, although she wasn't even sure how long ago they had died. If it was relatively recent, then that could be part of his touchiness. Joel had told her he'd been on his own and in shelters for the last few years, though, so it couldn't have been that recent. It was sad that he ended up on the streets after they died. She couldn't imagine not having anyone else he could have turned to in all this time. Then again, she had no idea how much of that was his choice.

What frustrated her the most was that if she just understood more about his past, and it was really as bad as she supposed, then it would go a long way toward excusing his current behavior. But since she was in the dark, she wasn't sure how mad she should be at him.

Was he acting unreasonably and just being a jerk? Or was there a very good reason he was so touchy about things like money, debt and his family. She was his girlfriend, for god sakes. *Wait, was she?* They never really had a conversation about it. She wanted to bring it up a few times, but she was always concerned about how he would react. The truth was, she wasn't sure at all what he felt about their relationship.

She resolved to bring it up the next time she saw him, whenever that was. He was already pissed off at her anyway, she may as well get this subject out there as well and deal with it all at once. It would help to know where she stood. After all, if he was just thinking about her as a fun little diversion, or a place to sleep where he didn't have to worry about getting robbed in the night, then it was better to end it now anyway. But she hoped she was more than that. A lot more.

According to the clock next to her bed, Joel's training should just be starting. Neither of them had any idea how long it would go, but now it sounded like he wasn't even planning on returning when it was finished.

Fuck him. She had to work tonight anyway. Friday night was a big tip night, and the money was always needed. Still, tips often reflected the frame of mind she was in, which meant that by the end of the night she might actually owe somebody money. Guys typically wanted their hot bartender to be perky and friendly and flirt with them. If any of them so much as made a comment about her mood tonight, though, they'd be lucky not to end up with a drink in their face.

She needed a distraction. Someone or something to take her mind off of Joel for the night. Her mind immediately went to her gay bar-back, Simon. He was always asking her to go to an after-hours place to get shit faced once their night ended, but she was usually too tired. But she had no reason to run home tonight, or to get up early tomorrow morning. Better to sleep away a hangover than deal with obsessive thoughts about where Joel was and whether he was still mad at her.

Amber got back into bed and pulled her sheet up to her chin, despite the heat in the apartment. If she was going to go out late tonight, she could use a nap. She was up too early this morning, giving out surprise shower blow jobs. Look how well that turned out. She closed her eyes, waiting for sleep to lull her back into unconsciousness. At least then she could stop thinking about Joel and the oversized chip on his shoulder.

CHAPTER THIRTY-FOUR
JOEL

Joel showed up about 20 minutes early to Rock House, carrying his workout and sparring gear in an old knapsack slung over one shoulder. He was impressed as soon as the building was in sight.

Rock House was a massive structure. It looked to be a converted warehouse, with the outside painted a dark and textured gray that he assumed was supposed to make it look like stone. In front of it was a huge sign on a pole at least 50 feet in the air. Rock House Training Center - Mixed Martial Arts.

Joel pushed past the big double doors and was immediately hit by the familiar smell of sweat and heavy, wet air. He breathed it in deeply, finding it strangely comforting and hoping it would help him relax a bit and shake off the fatigue and overall grumpiness that he was still feeling after his restless night and early argument.

Inside was just as impressive as outside. The place was huge, made up for the most part of a vast open area with simple thin mats along the floor. At the back, he could see a full size MMA style octagon cage, as well as a regular wrestling ring next to it. On the opposite end, there was work out equipment. Mostly free weights, but a few bikes for cardio as well. Draped along one of the walls was an immense American flag.

It was also immediately clear that not everyone was told to start at nine. There were at least fifteen guys in the place. Some of them had obviously just gotten there and were standing around talking, but others were already working out. A couple were sparring on the mat, some others were using the equipment and one was pounding on one of the many heavy bags that hung along the perimeter of the big open space.

His eyes were wide as he scanned the room, still taken aback by how immense it was. He wondered how much a place like this would cost to train at if he had to pay. Certainly more than he could ever afford. He gritted his teeth as it reminded him of how much he really owed to Amber that you couldn't really put a price on. If it wasn't for her, he wouldn't be here. He was a fool for taking out his frustrations on her this morning. That was definitely no way to start repaying his debt.

"Joel!"

He turned to see Shawn Rock walking toward him. The big MMA former champion grasped his hand and shook it firmly in greeting. "Good to see you. How's the head?"

Joel instinctively lifted his hand up to reach around and touch the injury which had now healed over pretty well. Shawn had sent the team doctor over to Amber's place the night after the tournament and he had confirmed it was a concussion, albeit a very minor one. He had been more concerned about the cut at the back of his head, putting in five stitches to close it up, telling him to wait ten to twelve days to fight again. Joel had pushed to start as soon as he could. Today was the earliest he was cleared. "Great," he said.

"Cool, cool. Okay, well let's introduce you to a few people and then get you started." Shawn motioned with his head for Joel to follow and he walked over to the group of men that weren't training yet. There were four of them standing together and talking. They stopped as the two men approached. A couple of them nodded at Shawn. One of them looked at Joel as if he'd just bitten into a lemon.

"Boys, this is Joel Slater, the guy I was telling you about that shoulda won that Golden Dragon tournament. Lucky for us he didn't and we stole him away from Tiger Strike. He has a keen eye for weaknesses in his opponents, so watch out what you show him." Shawn laughed, as did a couple of others. Sour mouth just glared at Joel.

"Anyway, this here is Chris Leeman," Shawn patted a broad shouldered man who had short, curly blond hair that was streaked with red dye. Chris reached forward and shook Joel's hand.

"Kingston West," Shawn said, putting his hand on the shoulder of a large black man. He was even taller than Joel by at least 2 inches, and had muscles of midnight stretching his tight white T-shirt. He smiled without showing any teeth, giving a little nod in Joel's direction.

"Rorie McMahon." Rorie was shorter than Joel, and leaner as well. But his body was sinewy and tight, without an ounce of fat to be seen. He had short red hair and hard green eyes.

"Hey," he said.

"Hi."

"And finally, Blake Edwards." Sour puss took a quick look at Shawn and then nodded at Joel, but as soon as Shawn turned away his face curled back into a sneer. Blake looked to be about Joel's height, but thicker. He was bald, with tattoos running up and down both of his arms, likely extending to the rest of his upper body as well but they were obscured by his shirt.

"I've asked these guys to come in today to help show you the ropes around here, they're all part of my core group that I have the highest hopes for in terms of making it all the way. Don't be surprised if you see any of these guys fighting on TV pretty soon. Hell, you'll probably see all of them eventually. It's somewhere I think you can get to as well, Joel." Shawn started to walk. "Come on, let me show you the locker room."

The two men left the group of fighters and walked to a set of doors near the back. Shawn opened one up and motioned Joel through, following after him. The locker room was fairly small, but it still held about 50 lockers. Attached was a washroom and a few shower stalls.

"Just find a place to store your stuff and put on your gear. Head on out to the guys and they'll get you started. Like I said, I expect good things from you, Joel. Rock House is one of the hardest gyms around, but we get results. I've brought half a dozen guys up from nothing to fighting at the highest levels in the last six months alone. But you have to put in the time. Two or three times a week isn't going to cut it here. I expect you to be here five, maybe six times if you expect to get results."

"No problem," Joel said. He had no intention of slacking. This was his dream, and he wasn't planning on fucking it up."

"Cool, cool," Shawn said, turning back to the door and pulling it open. "One more thing, though. I know you got that injury fighting with an underground club. That stops immediately. You fight with Rock House, at Rock House, or where Rock House tells you to fight. Training here means not jeopardizing yourself anywhere else. We're putting time and resources into your body, and it's no longer yours to risk - not if you want to continue with us, anyway. Understood?"

Joel nodded. "Of course."

Shawn nodded and then left.

That would be a problem.

CHAPTER THIRTY-FIVE
AMBER

"What the hell are you doing here this early, girl?"

"Before you start on me, I brought you a Frappuccino, so choose your words carefully."

Simon's eyebrows melted into his hairline and a smile spread across his face as he reached to snatch the drink from Amber's hands. "I was just going to say what a pleasure it is to see you in here so long before your shift," he said slowly.

Amber laughed. "You're a terrible liar."

"You caught me off guard. Try giving me a morning to come up with a reason for why I'm late for work instead of admitting to just being hung over, then we'll talk. If you can still accuse me of that, I'll get to see how good a liar *you* are." Simon sniffed and took a sip of his drink, trying to look hurt but his eyes betrayed his cheerfulness. She didn't know if she had ever seen him in a bad mood, or even a very serious one for that matter, which was why she had come in early. Simon could always cheer her up when she was bummed about a guy. He had more experience with them than she had, after all.

"Seriously though," he said after putting his cup down. "It's not even one o'clock. You don't start for another four hours."

"I was tired of staring at the walls and being pissed off," she said, plopping her bag down against the bar and sliding onto a stool. It was rare she got to see the bar from this perspective.

"Oh, oh. What did fight club do now?"

Amber stuck her tongue out at Simon. She hated when he called Joel that. "Nothing. I don't know. We got in a fight and he stormed out, I don't even know when or if he'll be home tonight. "

"About what?"

"Money, I think. Honestly, I don't even know for sure. One minute I'm asking him to move in with me and the next minute he's basically accusing me of being a gold digger. I don't get him at all. He's so touchy, especially about money."

"Probably because he never has any. Didn't you find him sleeping on a park bench or something?

"No, stop it," she said, swatting at his arm. Simon just smiled and spun out of reach, taking another sip of his frap.

"Listen, I'm just saying they don't get much poorer than him. Wouldn't it be nice to date someone with money for a change? Someone who can take care of you instead of needing you to mother him?"

"I don't care about money," she said. Simon did, and he couldn't understand when other people didn't. He once told her he would never date a man who didn't own a BMW or Jaguar. She wasn't sure if he was kidding or not, it wasn't always easy to tell with him.

"Well, you might not, but how do you know what he really wants. Maybe his whole money issue thing is some sort of over compensation defense type thing because in reality, he's after your money."

"What money, doctor Freud?"

"Well, your potential money."

"I work at a bar, I don't think there's a lot of danger of me attracting any Bernie Madoff type suitors."

"Don't sell yourself short, girl. You're still young. This isn't your last stop."

"Whatever. Anyway, he's not like that."

"How do you know," Simon said, walking back over to her and leaning against the bar. "How well do you really know this guy, anyway? You've known him for what, like a week?"

"Two. But so what? He's private, that's all."

"People who are 'private' usually have something to hide."

Amber sighed. "Joel's not like that." *Is he?* He was extremely private, and never wanted to talk about his past at all. She got the feeling she wasn't even allowed to ask about it. Could he be hiding some deep dark secret? Even if he was, she didn't think it had anything to do with money. But there were worse secrets he could be keeping.

"Hey, you know who else was private and liked to keep to himself? Jeffrey Dahmer. That is, until he was hungry."

"Oh my god, Simon. Would you stop?"

"Listen, I'm just saying, there could be lots of reasons he doesn't want to talk about his past or his family. Like maybe he killed them all and is on the run, hiding out in shelters and fighting in back alleys to keep the voices from his head."

Amber put her hands over her ears. "STOP!"

Simon laughed and Amber reached over and grabbed the fountain gun, turning it on him and spraying him with water as he ran to the back of the bar. "Okay, okay, I'll stop. Truce!"

She put the gun back down and glared at her friend. "I came here so that you'd make me feel better, not so that you'd add to the crazy thoughts in my head."

He walked slowly back, shaking his shirt to peel the wet fabric from his body. "Okay, fine. What *do* you know about him?"

"Not very much. His name and... actually, I guess just his name."

Simon sighed and put a damp hand on the back of Amber's shirt. "You're lucky you have me in your life, that's all I have to say."

"Why?"

"This is the internet age. The age of information. You think I go out with a guy even once without cyber stalking his ass? If for no other reason than to check out his net worth and whether he's got a secret wife somewhere that he's closeted from? Not that that last part is a deal breaker, by the way."

Of course not. "So, you think you could find something out about him?"

"Girl, if I can't I'll be a lot more disappointed in myself than you'll be. Come on, there's a computer in the back office we can use." Simon started to walk away as he kept talking, not even waiting to see if Amber was following.

"Trust me, I haven't sucked a dick that didn't have six figures behind it since I left high school. If I can't find out something about fight club's past, then it's because he comes from Mars and doesn't have one. "

"Gross," she said, slipping off her stool and following her friend. *It can't hurt to just take a quick look. Just to make sure he isn't a lunatic.*

CHAPTER THIRTY-SIX
JOEL

The training began normally when Joel returned to the main gym. He rejoined the group of fighters that Shawn had introduced him to and they all ran through some simple warm ups. From sprints and rolls, to push ups and burpees. The actual warm up lasted for over thirty minutes and got progressively harder as time wore on. For the most part, Blake was leading the group in terms of what they did next, standing in front of them so that they could follow along with what he was doing. By the time they took a break, Joel was covered in a heavy layer of sweat. The other guys didn't seem quite as winded.

He was taking a sip from his water bottle, letting his heart rate come down a bit, when he felt a hand rest on his shoulder. It was Chris Leeman. "Feel the burn yet?" he asked with a smile. He was missing a tooth along his bottom row.

Joel nodded. "Good work out. It always like that?"

Chris shrugged as his hand slipped off Joel's shoulder and he grabbed his own water. "I think Blake was putting on a bit of a show for you today."

Joel grunted. It didn't surprise him, given the way Blake had glared at him earlier. He wasn't sure what that guy's problem was, but he wasn't going to let him get under his skin. He glanced over his shoulder to see whether the other fighter was nearby, but he was only bending over at one of the benches and grabbing his own drink, facing away from the two of them. When he stood up, Joel did a double take.

"What the fuck is that?"

"What?" Chris asked. He followed Joel's gaze and then laughed. "I think it's for intimidation, but whenever I see it, all I can think about is that he's thick headed, or a blockhead." Chris laughed again but then quickly added "But don't tell him I said that. I'll deny the shit out of it."

They were looking at a tattoo stenciled onto the back of Blake's head. It was very detailed, and was made to look as if a circular bit of his skull had broken off and underneath was a red brick wall.

Joel smiled at Chris's comment as he shook his own head. "I guess some people just know that MMA is going to be their life forever."

"What do you mean?"

"I'm just saying, the way he's tattooed his whole body, he's not going to be applying for any office jobs. He's pretty much committed himself to his craft."

Chris smiled broadly, slapping Joel on the back again and then putting his water down. "Yep, I think you're right about that. Some people are just born to be bad-asses. But hey, isn't that why we're here, too? Anyway, come on, let's get back."

Joel put his own water down and turned to follow the fighter back to where the other three guys were starting to assemble again. *Am I any better than Blake? No tattoos, but I have no future other than fighting either.* Maybe the only difference between the two men was that Blake accepted his fate, embracing who he was while Joel always had the lingering doubt that he barely even knew himself.

The men started to lightly spar after donning their protective gear, pairing up while taking turns sitting one of them out to rest and act as ref when needed. Joel and Chris faced off, circling while they gauged each other's style. When they came together, they were evenly matched, with no man seeming to gain any advantage before time was called for a switch.

Joel next fought with Kingston. The big man nodded to him when they started, reaching his long arm out to touch knuckles lightly before leaping forward immediately and catching Joel on the side of the head with a punch. It knocked his head back, but he stayed on his feet, most of the sting from the hit being absorbed by his padded helmet.

Kingston was more aggressive than Chris, and Joel was forced to take a more defensive stance. He was able to parry the rest of the black man's attacks, but he hardly had time to throw anything of his own. He was both surprised and impressed with how quick his opponent could move, relative to his size. By the time their pair up was over, Joel was winded and happy to hear that it was his turn to sit out.

He sat on the side waiting for his heart rate to settle as he watched the other four men continue to spar. He was still tired from his lack of sleep the night before, and out of shape from the previous two weeks of what almost amounted to bed rest, his only exercise being the frequent naked wrestling matches that Amber usually initiated. He smiled as he thought about this morning and how she had greeted him in the shower.

How did I manage to even fuck that one up? She didn't deserve his outburst. Obviously Amber wasn't after his money, and he knew she wasn't making a subtle accusation that he needed to start paying rent. Yet he wasn't the kind of guy that needed her to point it out. *What kind of man needs a woman to put a roof over his head? You're a pussy, and you always were.* His father's voice raged in his head as if he were standing right next to him. The old man was right, as infrequent as that was.

He needed to contribute, and the only way he could see to do that was to find Randy and see if he could line up another underground match. He may have lost his last one, but he wouldn't be distracted this time. He could forget that one loss and return to his unbeaten status, building up a bankroll big enough to at least contribute to the rent. One or two fights a month should do it. No one would have to know.

"Joel, you coming or what?"

He shook his head to clear his thoughts. Blake was standing above him, glaring down. "You're with me," he said.

Leaping to his feet with a surge of adrenaline that hid how tired he was, Joel followed sour puss to the center of the mats, his eyes drawn to the unique tattoo. What had Chris called him? Blockhead? Maybe that fit better than sour puss. Joel was curious to find out just how thick his skull was. When Blake stopped and turned, Joel gave him a tight smile and nod but the other man just grimaced in return. "Show me why you get a free pass," he said, and then he lunged forward.

Joel put his arms out to stop Blake as he came forward, but the more experienced fighter dropped his shoulder at the last moment, catching Joel in the stomach and blasting the breath from his lungs as he flew backward. He instinctively grabbed onto the other man's back in order to keep from being knocked completely off his feet, but Blake's arms wrapped around his waist and he felt a leg swing around behind him. The full weight of his opponent pushed against him, tripping him and then landing hard on top of his body as they crashed into the mats. The back of his helmeted head bounced as it hit the ground, quickly met by Blake's elbow from the top.

Raising his arms to protect his head without thinking, Joel knew he was in trouble when he felt Blake push his arm against his face and slip his own around the back of Joel's head. He'd foolishly put himself in a position where his opponent could apply an arm triangle, and he had been too dazed and tired to foresee it, much less defend against it. As Blake squeezed, Joel had no choice but to tap out before he lost consciousness, although he did wait until the edges of his vision started to blacken before doing so.

Blake waited a fraction of a second longer than he needed to before he loosened his grip. He slid his arm out from under Joel and grunted. "Fucking joke, like I thought."

CHAPTER THIRTY-SEVEN
AMBER

"Look, right here, isn't this them?"

Amber squinted at where Simon was pointing on the screen. It was the obituary listings of the city newspaper but standing behind her friend she was too far away to read it.

"Oh wait, maybe not. When did you say they died?"

"I don't know, a few years ago I guess. Or longer."

"Okay, this can't be them then. Strange, though. The names match."

Amber pushed Simon aside and bent over his left shoulder to peer down at the screen.

SLATER, Darryl - Died as a result of injuries sustained in a motor vehicle accident. Darryl, 53, leaves behind wife Linda. Visitation to be held at Heavenly Bodies funeral chapel on August 14th from 2-4 with service to follow.

It was true, the names did match but there was no mention of Joel, and this paper was from last summer. Joel was already living on the streets then. Plus, it said that his mother was still alive.

"Pretty short compared to most of these others," Simon mused.

Amber nodded. You pay by the word, so it was likely short to save money. Simple, just to let friends and family know what happened and when and where to pay respects. It was quite a coincidence that both the husband and wife had the same first and last names as Joel's parents. And she knew that they didn't have a lot of money, either.

Simon started scrolling through his search results, looking for another match.

Was it possible that this was them? If so, why would Joel have lied about them being dead? Or at least of his mother being dead? Or did he *think* he was lying about them both? He'd been in shelters for longer than a year. Joel didn't seem to be the type of person that sat around reading the obituaries.

"Well, I don't see any others that match. We may have to look somewhere else. You sure he said they were dead, right?"

Amber thought back to her conversation the night that she met Joel.

"*Does your family know you do this?*" she had asked him, referring to the back alley fighting he was participating in to pay the bills.

"*They're all gone. No one to tell,*" he had said.

"*Oh, I'm sorry.*"

That was it. He never actually said they were dead, but he hadn't said anything to contradict the fact that she had obviously believed that to be the case.

"Can you look up any other info on that couple?" she asked suddenly.

Simon shrugged. "Well, the obit says it was a car accident, so maybe it made the news, let me see." His fingers started to fly across the keyboard as he began a new search.

Why would Joel want people to believe that his parents were dead? Obviously he had no intention of ever speaking to them again, if that were true. Why not just tell people that he had a falling out with them, or whatever secret it was that kept them apart. Were they embarrassing? All parents were, as far as Amber was concerned. Addicts? Criminals? Her mind raced at all of the possible reasons. What would cause her to stop talking to her own parents? To claim they were dead to anyone who asked?

"Here," Simon exclaimed, pointing at the screen again. This time there was a black and white photograph with a caption underneath that she couldn't read, and then an article. The headline read *Drunk driver killed on way home from liquor store.*

Amber bent forward again, her eyes quickly scanning the article. A shocking chill ran down her back as she read a line from the investigation. "The driver, now identified as Darryl Slater, leaves behind a wife and one estranged son, according to neighbors."

"Can you show me on a map where this accident happened?" Amber's heart was pounding in her chest and she put a hand on Simon's shoulder as a wave of dizziness rushed through her.

Simon opened up a map and zoomed in on the location from the article. There was no doubt about it now. The crash happened in the same neighborhood that Joel had mentioned growing up in.

"That's them," she said. She took a few steps backwards and flopped down on another chair. She was positive.

"So he lied about his mother being dead, but told the truth about his father?" Simon asked, spinning his chair to face her with a raised eyebrow.

"I think he lied about them both. This accident happened after he had left. I'm not sure he even knows about this."

"Who lies about their parents being dead?"

Amber shrugged. "Actually, he didn't lie. Not exactly. I don't know."

Simon stood up and then turned to turn off the browser in an effort to obscure what they had just been looking at before their boss came in. "Your boy has issues, you know that, right hon?"

Amber didn't answer as she thought about whether or not to tell Joel about this. Or how. He wasn't going to be happy that she looked him up in the first place. But how could she keep information like this to herself?

"Anyway, I gotta get back to work or you're not going to have any drinks to serve tonight." He put a hand on her shoulder and gave it a little squeeze. "You okay?"

She smiled slightly and nodded up at him with a sigh. "I think I might need a drink after work tonight. Or three."

Simon's face split into a wide grin. "Now you're talking girl! That's a fabulous idea. Drink away the pain. I know just the place." Her friend almost skipped out of the room, the heaviness of the past few minutes already fading from his carefree mind as she sunk lower into her chair, the smile fading from her lips.

Maybe he didn't want to know. After all, he wanted people to believe they were dead, so could it be that he wished they were? She couldn't imagine how she'd feel if someone kept information like that from her, though. She'd be devastated. But Joel was a very different person. What would be worse to him? Finding out that his father was dead, or that Amber had gone digging into his past.

She took a deep breath, letting it out slowly. She had a feeling she was in a no-win situation. The only way to avoid it would be to keep it from him completely, act like she never discovered it. Maybe she could somehow get him to find the article on his own or something. Then see how he reacted. Would he even tell her? Tears misted her vision. She knew the answer to that.

Amber leaned her head back against the wall, taking another deep breath to steady herself as she blinked away the half formed tears. Drinking tonight was a good idea. She could figure all of this out in the morning. Saying anything right away would be a rash decision. She needed to think about it for a while and figure it out. Besides, she had no idea when she would next see Joel anyway.

CHAPTER THIRTY-EIGHT
JOEL

Joel emerged from the underground into the sweltering night. The heat of the day hadn't yet dissipated despite it being after 10 P.M, but it was still better than the stifling and stagnant sweat filled air of Rock House after an entire day of training. The shower he had taken before leaving seemed pointless now, since even the short walk to Amber's apartment would undo all of its work. He could have another one once he got in, but with the way her air conditioning worked, it wouldn't last very longer either.

He was exhausted. Training had been brutal - much harder than he had anticipated, although Chris had confirmed that Blake was leading it harder than usual. Still, none of the other guys seemed as beat by the end of the night, and he knew he had a lot of work to do to get into shape. Those guys had been at it for months, some of them years. They knew what they were doing, but he was anxious to learn. Pain and exhaustion were welcome if they were harbingers of future success in the ring. Of the four men he was training with, three of them had already fought in televised events. It was even rumored that Blake was only a few fights away from a title shot himself.

He still wasn't sure what Blake's issue was with him. Each time the two of them sparred, he would shake his head or sneer every time he took Joel down or submitted him. Other than that, he barely spoke to him at all. At least the other guys hadn't been complete assholes. Chris was the most friendly. Joel definitely wasn't there to make friends, but if he was going to be spending almost every day with these guys, it would be nice if they were all at least civil to each other.

He reached the door and unlocked it with the extra key that Amber had loaned him. It was hours before she was due home, but that would give him time to decide what to say to her. How to apologize. He grimaced to himself. He could recall his father's claim, many times growing up. *Apologies are for weaklings.* He never once heard the man apologize for anything, and if anyone had anything to be sorry for, it should be Darryl Slater.

The door of the elevator opened for Joel and he pressed seven as he walked in and leaned against the back wall, closing his eyes and trying to banish thoughts of his father from his mind. Thinking of him rarely led to anything good, only serving to make his blood boil. If he was going to apologize to Amber he needed to remain calm and level headed.

Closing his eyes only served to remind him how tired he was, though. He almost missed the doors as they started to close at his floor, only saving himself from another trip to the lobby by hastily thrusting his arm in between and letting them crash into him and then rebound as they sensed an obstruction. By the time he had made his way into the apartment, he had forgotten about his desire to shower and clean the fresh film of sweat from his body and instead flopped down onto the couch to wait for Amber.

The apartment was still hot, the AC still not working properly. Joel offered to talk to the landlord to try and convince him to fix it, but Amber had an idea of what type of persuasive techniques he'd be tempted to try so she dissuaded him. She'd been right, of course. He needed to stop trying to solve problems with his fists. Breaking that lifelong habit would be tough.

As much as he wanted to help and contribute, get out of the debt he felt like he owed to her, he was starting to rethink his decision to go back and fight for Randy. His whole life no one had really earned his respect the way Amber had. She gave selflessly and the only thing she had really asked of him was that he give up those underground matches because they were too dangerous.

It was odd to him, having someone care about him the way that she did. He'd never had that feeling before, even from his own parents. Amber respected him, his quirks and his temper, his obsessive need for privacy about his past, his touchiness about money and debt. If all she really wanted in return for all of that was to know that he was safe and not getting his ass kicked in an alley somewhere, he should do his best to just give that to her. There was very little else that was within his power to give. He wasn't sure what he'd done to deserve someone like her in his life, but he found himself wanting to finally trust her. It was a relief to finally have someone like that in his life.

He was still going over it in his mind when exhaustion finally overtook his senses, snatching consciousness away from him and replacing it with a deep and dreamless slumber.

CHAPTER THIRTY-NINE
AMBER

Amber ran through the dark house, chasing after Joel but each time her fingers came closer to catching him, he would seem to dissolve between her fingers and run a different way. "Missed!" he said.

Her feet were moving faster now, but the walls were tilting back and forth as if the whole house were teetering on its edge. First one way, then the opposite. Joel ran by and she tried for him again. He slipped through her right hand but then her left swung around. That was too late as well.

"Miss, miss," he taunted. Why couldn't she hold onto him?

"Miss?"

Amber jumped as a hand touched her shoulder. "Miss, we're here. $23.50."

She blinked a few times as she let reality sink in and ground her. The cab driver's weathered hand snaked back through the plexiglass divider between them. He didn't look very happy at having to wake up his fare.

"Sorry," Amber mumbled. She reached into her purse and withdrew a twenty and a ten, pushing it through the hole he had just used to wake her up. "Keep the change." That elicited a smile at least. It had been an expensive ride for her, but Simon had insisted and she was glad he had. The subway wasn't running at this time of night anyway, and the all night bus would have been packed with drunks and nutcases, with the occasional psychopath hidden in the mix.

Stumbling out of the car and fumbling with her keys, she made it inside her security door as her taxi pulled away, anxious to return to a more affluent neighborhood. The walls of the elevator on her way up to the seventh floor seemed to wobble just like in her dream, and for a moment she had to concentrate not to throw up. Simon had a much higher tolerance for Jager Bombs than she did. But it was so worth it. She hadn't had that much fun in a long time.

Still smiling, Amber pushed open the door to her apartment and threw her purse down, kicking it closed with her foot and turning the lock as she laughed at memories of Simon trying to start up a karaoke session at the bar. It seemed funny at the time, at least to them - but not as much to everyone else in the bar. Now that she was starting to sober up, she could see how some of the other patrons had probably just found them annoying.

The quick nap in the cab had helped to push away most of her drunkenness, years of working in a bar and sneaking the shots that flirting customers had bought her gave her the ability to rebound fairly quickly after a night of drinking, even though she still often felt nausea and instability on her feet until the next morning.

Stumbling toward the bedroom to sleep the rest of it off, she stopped dead as she passed the couch. "Joel! What the fuck are you doing here?"

The well built fighter lying on her couch didn't stir, his chest rising and falling steadily.

Giving in to an overwhelming urge to sit, Amber plopped down onto the couch next to Joel's chest, causing him to bounce on the cushions and then snap awake.

"What? What's happened. Where... oh. Hi." He shook his head, shaking off the remains of the deep sleep he'd just been pulled from.

"I thought you weren't..." Amber paused as a wave of nausea fluttered through her stomach. "...coming home tonight," she finished.

"I know. Look..." Joel started to say something and then trailed off.

"Whatever," Amber said, smiling. "I'm glad you came home. I had the best time tonight. I went out with Simon and he took me to a gay bar and it was so much fun oh my god. We tried to sing on stage, well, it wasn't really a stage but there was this-"

"Amber," Joel said, holding up his hand to stop her. She paused, still smiling at him. He was again quiet for a moment, lost in thought. Does he know who Simon is? *Does he think I'm cheating or something?*

"Simon's just my gay friend," she explained. "I wanted to go drinking tonight and he always goes drinking after work. He works behind the bar with me. He's so funny, you should totally meet-"

Joel held up a hand again. "I don't care about Simon," he said. "I wanted to talk to you about something else." Joel's eyes narrowed and he pursed his lips. "It's about earlier. I shouldn't have gone off like that. I know you... I know you were just trying to help. I know you aren't after money or anything. I just... the one thing I learned from my parents was to never be in anyone's debt."

He was trying to apologize, and Amber thought it was sweet until he mentioned his parents. As soon as he did, she remembered the lie she had discovered earlier and she wrinkled her nose at him. "Your parents? You mean the ones that died years ago that you never want to talk about?" Her resolution not to bring it up until she had time to think about it evaporated faster than the Jager bombs in front of Simon.

Joel sat up on the couch, but he looked away. "There isn't anything to say about them."

"So you're still going with the story that they're dead?"

Joel's head snapped around as he looked at her sharply, but he said nothing. Her lips had a mind of their own.

"I know you lied about them," she said. "Simon and I looked them up." Anger flared in her chest as the accusation burned through her, but then she suddenly remembered what else they had found. Immediately she could feel tears welling up in her eyes, the alcohol taking her on a roller coaster of emotions. "Oh, Joel..." she sighed, but he was barely listening to her now as his own anger began to bubble to the surface.

"What do you mean, you looked them up?" he asked, the words falling from his mouth one at a time.

"On the computer," she said. Big tears were forming and she had to blink to hold them back. "But we found something else out," she said.

"What the fuck, Amber? Who told you to go and look my past up?"

"Joel, would you calm down for a minute? You said they were dead. I just wanted to find out the details so I could understand-" She put her hand on his chest but he shook her off and pulled his legs up and off the couch. Leaping to his feet he turned back and glared at her.

"I never said they were dead!"

"Yes you did, you told me that your parents had been gone for years."

"Right. Gone. I never said dead. They were gone from my life. They might as well be dead. They're dead to me. But that still gives you no right-"

"Joel, would you stop for a minute!" she said. She reached out and grabbed his hand, giving it a squeeze. "Listen, we found something else. About your father."

"I don't care, Amber," he said, pulling his hand away from hers. "I fucking told you, they're dead to me. I don't give a shit what you found out."

Amber stared at Joel, the tears falling from her eyes freely now. Something about her look gave him pause, his anger seeming to disperse slightly at her raw emotion. "What?" he demanded.

"Your father. I'm sorry Joel. He really is dead."

She watched as his face became an emotionless mask, the color draining from it slightly. His hands, which had been hanging loosely by his waist, slowly pulled themselves closed into tight fists.

CHAPTER FORTY
JOEL

The news of his father hit Joel like a roundhouse kick to the head, momentarily making him forget his anger at Amber's betrayal of his privacy. Darryl was dead? He didn't believe it.

"What are you talking about?" he asked slowly. His body was rigid as he stood there, and he realized that his fists were clenched tightly at his sides. He loosened them and took a deep breath to steady himself. Amber was drunk, she probably didn't know what she was talking about. How would she even know how to find his parents, anyway?

Tears were falling from her eyes and she stepped forward again, now that he wasn't making fists, and grabbed one of his hands, pulling it close to her chest. "Oh Joel, I'm so sorry. I wasn't sure if you knew. I know I shouldn't have been looking them up but Simon was saying that I didn't know anything about you and that he could just look them up quickly and-"

"What did you find," he asked, cutting off her drunken rambling. He was losing patience with her and he pulled his hand back.

She paused, looking down at the hand he had yanked away like it was a snake that had just struck her and retreated. He instantly felt guilty but pushed that emotion aside. She was the one who should feel guilty for betraying his trust.

"Simon found his obituary in an old newspaper archive online. At first I didn't know it if it was him, but it mentioned your mother Linda, by name. But then they didn't say anything about you in it so we looked a little further and-"

"How?" he snapped. It surprised him more that there had been an obituary in the newspaper at all than the fact that he wasn't mentioned. Then again, his mother always seemed to have some sick sense of devotion to that malicious fuck, so maybe that was her way of giving him a respectful send off. He couldn't imagine who would have cared though, neither of them really had any close friends.

"A car accident, he was... well, I don't know if it was true but-"

"Drunk?" he finished for her. That sounded like his father alright.

Amber just nodded, her big eyes looking warily at him, likely waiting for some sort of breakdown or reaction. If she was expecting an explosion of tears, she'd be disappointed. He felt more angry than anything. But why? *I've wished that fuck was dead more times than I can count, why should I be angry that it's finally true?*

"When was this?"

"Last summer," she said. Her voice was just a whisper now. She still watched him, but made no more moves to touch him or approach.

Joel realized his hands were back into tight balls, pressed against his hips. The blood in his veins raced through him, pulling tension and fury to each of his extremities. He still had no idea why this news filled him with so much rage. Unable to determine the true source, he finally settled on focusing on Amber's betrayal as a surrogate.

"You had no right to invade my privacy," he said through his teeth. His past was his and his alone. He wasn't proud of it, and he never chose to share any more of it than he had to with anyone. The fact that Amber and some stranger had dug around in some computer looking up details of his life filled him with apprehension. His parents had never had any sort of computer growing up, and his school only had them in the library. Shelters were more concerned with food and beds than technology. Computers were an unknown entity to him. He hadn't ever imagined they could also be used to delve into his personal history and spill his secrets.

"Joel, I'm so sorry about your father..."

"Are you kidding me?" he asked, his rage flaring out as he sneered at her. "You think I give two shits that that sick fuck is dead? Didn't your fucking computer tell you how Darryl used to beat the shit out of my mother and me? Didn't it tell you how they kicked me out as soon as I was 18 with just the clothes on my back, happy to finally get rid of me?"

"No!" Amber cried out. "Joel, I'm sorry. I had no idea. We just saw the news about your parents and I thought you should know."

Joel felt his face get hot as he realized it was his own admission now that was revealing the shame of his past, but he pushed past it. Amber needed to hear these things, needed to know that he was unlovable, even to his parents. She was too good a person to get wrapped up in his life.

"Well, now you know. I learned to fight because of him. I learned how to take a punch, and how to deal with pain. Maybe I at least have that to thank him for. He also taught me that no one can be trusted." He glared in Amber's direction. "That's one lesson I should have paid more attention to."

"Joel-"

"I don't want to hear it!" he growled. The look on his face made Amber take a step back, causing an instant blast of remorse to well up in his stomach. He swallowed that feeling back as well. "Coming back here was a mistake," he said, a bit softer this time. He shook his head as he looked around the little apartment, purposely avoiding eye contact with Amber. If he saw her tears, he might soften the decisions that were forming in his mind.

This was no place for him. Amber was too naive. They had nothing in common. She didn't *get* him, and she never would.

He'd been alone for years, and that's the way he needed to stay. Otherwise someone would get hurt. And he cared too much about Amber to let that someone be her.

"I don't know if this relationship is the best idea," he said. He stared at the floor between them as he spoke.

"What do you mean?" Amber's voice was quivering.

"I'm worried you're going to get hurt."

"Don't you think that risk is mine to take?" she replied, her voice taking on a more defiant tone.

He lifted his eyes from the floor to meet her gaze. She was glaring at him, her eyes red from alcohol and tears.

"Are you worried about me, or yourself?" she asked.

He frowned at her. "What's that supposed to mean?"

"You're Mr. Fight Club," she said, borrowing Simon's nickname. "You can take a punch or get your head slammed into a brick wall and shrug everything off. But when it comes time to stick your neck out emotionally, you run away scared. Every fucking time."

"That's bullshit. I just don't want to feel responsible when this whole relationship comes crashing down. Because it will. That's what always happens."

"Blah, blah. Stop feeling sorry for yourself, Joel," she said. She put a hand on her hip and was leaning forward but he noticed her other hand holding onto the couch to keep her steady. "You've had a hard life. I get it. Your parents were assholes, I get it. But when are you going to stop using that as an excuse to keep from getting on with your life? Stop living under the shadow of your past!"

"You don't know anything about me," he spat.

"I know!" she said, her voice rising an octave as she practically shook. "Because you won't fucking tell me anything! So yes, I had to go look it up for myself. Forgive me for giving a shit about my boyfriend and wanting to know more about him!"

Boyfriend? That wasn't something they had discussed, and he could see in her eyes as she said it that it was a slip of the tongue. But she didn't pause for long.

"I'm just saying, when two people are together they share things about their lives, Joel. You know way more about me than I know about you. Like the fact that I dream of being a nurse, but probably never will because I'll never be able to afford it working at a shitty bar job. Hell, I can't even afford a stethoscope. But at least I've told you my dreams. I've told you things about me that I've never told anyone. What have you told me, Joel? That your parents died a long time ago? I thought that was something. Turns out that was just a lie so that you wouldn't have to open up about them.

"So go ahead," she turned her body, moving herself out from between him and the door. "There's the door. Run away like you always do. Just don't expect that I'm going to be here every time to take you back. I'm getting tired of this shit. I want a commitment, Joel. I want some stability. And I think that would help you, too."

His eyes met hers and the two of them stared in silence at each other. "Fine," he said. Breaking their visual standoff, he walked past her without another glance and left.

She doesn't know what the fuck she's talking about anyway.

CHAPTER FORTY-ONE
AMBER

The sun streaming in from between the blinds sliced through Amber's eyelids and drilled into her brain, making it feel like it was splitting in half. With one heavy arm, she pulled her bed sheet over her head in an effort to shield herself, but the pain lessened only slightly.

What the fuck?

It took her longer than it should have to remember that she was hung over and not, in fact, in the middle of a brain aneurysm. Slowly, as she lay hidden in the humidity under the thin layer of cotton, the events of the night before began to seep back into her mind like a slow IV drip. Thoughts of Simon and drinking came first. Something about Karaoke. Waking up in a cab.

Joel.

The pounding of her chest grew as the details of their fight flooded back, the drip now becoming a torrent. He had come back to apologize and somehow she had let her little covert op with Simon slip out. And then she'd called him her boyfriend. She winced at that, but not half as much as when she remembered trying to bluff him into staying. She'd never been a very good poker player, and Joel had called her, walking out into the night once again.

She went over the events in her head again, more of the details filling in as the fogginess of the night was pushed away by adrenaline. She'd said things to Joel that she should have kept to herself. Things she'd been thinking lately, but never would have uttered if it hadn't been for the Jägermeister truth serum running through her veins.

Now who knows what would happen. Would he ever come back again? Should she go out looking for him and apologize? He was probably at the Rock House, or would head to a shelter near there for the night. He wanted privacy though. Wasn't that what the whole fight had been about? No, if he was going to come back it needed to be on his own. And she would just have to wait and see if he did.

She flipped the covers back over her head, releasing the trapped and stale air as cooler air from the apartment washed over her. The contrast was almost enough to let her imagine her air conditioner was working again, at least for the few seconds until she adjusted to the new temperature and started to feel hot again.

She rolled out of bed and pulled off her sweaty clothes as she headed for a shower. If she was going to accuse Joel of feeling sorry for himself, she should make sure she wasn't also guilty of it. She needed to take her mind off him and their issues for a little while, at least until it was time to go back to the bar. The fast paced and noisy environment there would definitely keep her from obsessing.

She veered off course and into the living room, picking up her phone and quickly dialing.

"Room 114 please," she said to the woman who answered. She waited patiently to be connected until she heard a familiar voice on the other end.

"Hi Nana," she said, raising her voice in case the older woman wasn't wearing her hearing aid. She tended not to wear it when she wasn't expecting company.

"Hello? Who is this?"

"It's Amber, Nana."

"Who?"

"Amber. Judith's daughter."

"Judy? Is that you?"

"No, it's Amber," she sighed. "Can I come for a visit today?"

"Of course, Judy dear. I'd love to see you. Is your brother coming as well?"

"No, just me," she said. "I'll be there in an hour."

"Okay dear."

She hung up the phone, a heaviness in her chest as she walked back to the bathroom and turned on the water. Her maternal grandmother had lived with her and her parents from the time Amber was 12, helping to raise her just as puberty was starting to confuse her world. Nana had always been a more calming and balanced presence than her own mother, her easy-going attitude a sharp contrast to her mother's exacting expectations. Her father had largely stayed out of most things, siding with her mother whenever he was put on the spot.

But then Alzheimer's had started when Amber was 15. At first, they didn't really notice it. Nana was in her seventies so it was normal that she would forget things. But then it got worse, and she started to mix people up or to find them completely unfamiliar - often forgetting Amber entirely or confusing her with her mother Judith. Soon she was disoriented and confused more often than not.

When Amber was 16, her grandmother fell down the stairs, breaking her hip. She never fully recovered from that, and needed a wheelchair from then on. It fell to Amber to take care of her at nights while her parents worked, having shifted their jobs around so that they were more available during the day while she was at school. She would help feed and bath her, show her pictures of the family and try to help her remember. Mostly she just spent time with her. It was during that time that she realized how much she enjoyed helping people, and considered becoming a nurse.

But after high school, her family didn't have much money since they had spent a lot of it on medical bills. Her father died of a heart attack when she was 18, and her mother ended up losing her job at around the same time. She was able to find another one pretty quickly, but it wasn't as flexible with the hours, even though it paid more. That meant that she wouldn't be around during the day, so Amber gave up on the idea of college altogether and got a job at the bar so she would be available for Nana until her mother came home.

Within a year, though, Nana had deteriorated too far, and was beyond her ability to care for properly. They'd had to move her into a home. When she left, so did Amber.

It had been too long since she'd been for a visit. It would be the perfect thing to get her mind off of Joel.

CHAPTER FORTY-TWO
JOEL

Joel got to Rock House just before 9 A.M. full of energy. He was glad he had slept for hours before Amber had come home, or he'd probably be a zombie today.

After their fight, he had headed over to Neutron's, the bar that Randy, the underground fight club organizer, usually frequented. When he had been fighting and winning, most of their nights would end at Neutron's where they would party until the wee hours of the morning. The only reason he came along was because Randy would always be buying, flush with the night's take from all of the bets. Joel could score some food and a couple of beers without having to dip into his own savings, and even when he had to fight the next day it was never until after dark, giving him plenty of time to rest.

Things hadn't changed, and Randy had been there celebrating with a few young fighters who Joel didn't recognize. Randy was happy to see Joel, and even happier when he told him he wanted to fight again. News about Joel's tournament at Golden Dragon had reached the promoter and he thought it would help spur some gambling on the man who had come so close to fighting Carlos Alvarez. Apparently Carlos had become a big deal around town as well, as he was slated to fight in a televised event for Titan, which was rumored to often be used as a farm league for some of the bigger players like the UFC, Strikeforce or PrideFC.

Randy told Joel that he could set up a fight for that very night, and Joel had jumped at the chance to earn some money again. He was also excited about being able to release some of his temper. Rock House would help with that as well, but it was far more satisfying to feel his bare knuckles slam into flesh than the bounce of the rubber gloves he had to wear during practice. He left soon after speaking with Randy and was able to get in almost three more hours of sleep, meaning he was rested and ready to go for training.

The other guys were already there and had started their warm-up by the time Joel met them at their corner of the mat.

"Got somewhere more important to be, Slater?" Blake asked as soon as the new fighter joined them.

"I thought we started at nine," he replied.

"We don't just do the bare minimum here, Slater. That might be what you're used to, but it doesn't fly at Rock House."

"Hey, why don't you go fuck yourself?" Joel shot back. He was in no mood for dealing with Blake being an asshole again.

Blake stopped what he was doing and walked forward, pressing his chest up against Joel. "You want to repeat that, you freeloading rookie?"

"Sure, why don't-"

"Guys, guys, come on," Chris said, wedging his hands between the two men and pushing them apart. "You know how Shawn feels about getting into personal fights. You want to get kicked out?"

Blake sneered at Joel and lifted his chin before turning on his heel. "Keep your mouth in line, Slater. Your training gear only protects your vitals."

Joel snorted at the veiled threat, opening his mouth to reply, but a warning glare from Chris made him swallow his retort. He was right. Blake wasn't worth getting kicked out. They could settle their differences when they were sparring.

Despite the fact that he had more distracting him today than he had yesterday, Joel was able to focus his anger and emotions into his session. Even still, when it came time to spar, he made sure to step up to Blake immediately to show the bigger man that he wasn't intimidated.

He could feel the eyes of the other fighters on them as they faced off, only half paying attention to their own matches.

As soon as they started, Blake lunged forward, just as he had last time. Joel hadn't forgotten that opener or the man's surprising speed, though, so he was ready. He moved quickly out of the way, throwing his elbow and catching Blake on the back as he passed. The big man turned back around to face him before Joel could do any other damage.

They began to circle now, with Blake more wary about his approach. All of a sudden, he threw a kick towards Joel's midsection which he barely dodged, but then followed it up with a quick jab that snapped his head back. Blake moved forward, trying to catch Joel before he had a chance to recover but Joel was ready, throwing his own right handed punch.

It was too slow, and Blake grabbed his extended arm with his left and pulled Joel off balance as he swung his other arm over Joel's shoulder, connecting both together into a kimura. His right leg hooked behind Joel and he tripped him as both men fell to the ground. Joel knew he was in trouble as Blake started to move the trapped arm sideways towards Joel's back. The pain of the arm lock was excruciating, but Joel resisted tapping out and instead put all of his energy into yanking his leg out from under Blake's in one explosive movement. As soon as it was free, he rolled forward, releasing his arm from the submission and dragging it out from under the bigger man.

He leapt on top of Blake, swinging his body around and into a full mount position, reversing the fortunes of the two men by giving himself the advantage now. From that position, he started to unleash his fists against the other man's helmeted head. In a typical fight, this would be pretty effective in quickly incapacitating an opponent, but between the gloves and the helmet he knew he wasn't really doing any real damage.

Blake then jerked his hips up, throwing Joel forward as his opponent slid out and brought his legs up, wrapping them around Joel who refused to be thrown off. Their positions had changed again and Blake was now in full guard. The two men spent the rest of the session in a stalemate until time was called by Kingston who was sitting out and watching.

Blake's legs loosened and Joel rolled out. As he did, he heard the other man grunt. "Better."

Joel didn't spar with Blake again for the rest of the day, instead spending most of his time working on submissions with Chris. By the time he left, it was time for dinner and he headed back to the shelter. With luck, he could get a quick meal there and then take a nap before his fight tonight. He had suggested the submission work to Chris today on purpose, knowing that working on arm bars and leg locks wouldn't leave him quite as exhausted as he had been last night after training, and it had worked. But he still wanted to rest so that he came to the fight ready to win.

CHAPTER FORTY-THREE
AMBER

"Hi Nana," Amber said as she opened the door to her grandmother's room. She had knocked but there was no answer. The elderly woman was sitting on a blue, Victorian style chair in the corner and looking out of the window to the courtyard of the home. There were some people out there, walking and talking. A little girl was laughing as she clung to the fingers of what was probably her grandfather.

Amber's grandmother turned, a look of confusion on her face as her brow furrowed. Some days she recognized her granddaughter and some days she didn't.

"Judy! How are you dear!" Today, it seemed as though she thought Amber was her mother again. It was easier to just play along than to try to explain it. Previous attempts had just left her heartbroken when she couldn't get through to her.

"I'm fine. Do you have your hearing aid in?"

"Oh, yes dear, it's right here." Nana reached over to the table beside her chair and picked up the small piece of plastic, bringing it up to her head and fastening it on her ear.

"It's good to see you," Amber said, once her grandmother could hear her properly.

"You, too, dear. Is Robert with you?" Robert was Amber's uncle, or had been, until he had died of cancer last year. It was another conversation she wasn't up for having yet again. "No, he couldn't make it."

Nana looked disappointed, but Amber had seen what she would look like when she found out he had died for the 100th time, and a little disappointment was much better. "Of course," the old woman said. "He's probably busy with the little ones."

The little ones were older than Amber now, but she just nodded.

"How have you been feeling?" she asked.

"Not bad," her grandmother responded. She always said the same thing. Nana didn't like to complain. She did look good, though. Amber was happy to see that this home was taking care of her, she still felt guilty at having to put her here.

"I wish I could have helped you more," she said, walking over and sitting down on the little bench next to her. Nana's hand was on the arm rest of her chair, so Amber reached over and placed hers on top, giving her grandmother a little squeeze.

"Of course, dear." She said that whenever she wasn't sure what the other person was talking about. It had started out when she was first diagnosed and trying to hide her deterioration from the family, but once it had taken hold the habit just stuck. These days, that phrase often made up the majority of their conversations.

"Are you still with that man, what's his name? Stanley?" Nana was stuck far in the past this time, Amber wasn't even aware of a Stanley in her dating history. But it was likely that Nana had latched on to the fact that Amber looked so young and her disease addled brain had placed her back 40 years or so, to when her own mother was young and dating. Amber smiled, recognizing the opportunity.

"No, I've met someone new. His name is Joel."

"Oh, that's nice dear. Does he treat you well?"

"Usually," she nodded. "But we're fighting at the moment."

"Oh, that's too bad. Well, you know when your father and I would fight, I would find that if I just apologized, that would usually fix things right up. Even if it was him that was in the wrong, which was most of the time." Her grandmother gave her a conspiratorial smile that Amber hadn't seen in a long time and she grinned back.

"It's a bit more complicated than that, I'm afraid. He left, I don't even know where he is."

"Hmph. Well, you know, if he's fool enough to leave a girl like you and not come back, then he's too big a fool for you."

Amber smiled. There was truth to that. She had only really known Joel for a couple of weeks, and as Simon had pointed out, she didn't even really *know* him. Why was she so smitten with him, anyway?

Her grandmother started to cough and Amber stood up, grabbing a tissue and holding it in front of her mouth. "Thank you, dear," Nana said.

"Nana, have you been eating?" Amber asked, noticing a tray of uneaten food on the dresser at the other end of the room.

"Of course, dear," she said. Amber frowned, unsure what that meant. Nana would often forget to eat when she had been taking care of her, and it got to the point where she would have to literally sometimes put the food right in her mouth to get her to remember that she was hungry. But once she could get her to put something in her mouth, it usually sparked her appetite.

She bent down and picked up the bag she had brought. "I brought you some things," Amber said, opening it up. Inside were mostly just an assortment of pictures, but there were also a few chocolates that her grandmother had always been fond of but rarely indulged in. She opened one up and gave it to her.

"My, what a treat," she said, popping the candy into her mouth. Amber smiled. At least she was eating something. The way Amber figured it, at 80 years old you were entitled to dessert first.

"Now, tell me about this boy," her grandmother said, smiling at her.

Amber laughed, happy that Nana was so interactive today. "Well, let's see. He's very handsome..." she began.

* * *

She stayed long enough to make sure that Nana ate her next meal and then Amber made her way to the bar for work. At the end of the night, she declined Simon's offer of a repeat of the previous nights festivities and raced home, anxious to see if Joel had returned again. Her heart felt heavy when she opened the door to an empty apartment.

He was obviously still upset. She felt sick to her stomach when she thought about some of the things he'd said, what he'd gone through. An abusive and alcoholic father, being kicked out by both parents and left with nothing and no one. No wonder he hadn't wanted to talk about his past. He was ashamed of it. But it made her sad to think that he felt that way. If only he had trusted her enough to confide in her, she could have told him it was nothing to be ashamed of, none of that was his fault.

But now it might be too late.

He taught me that no one can be trusted. That's one lesson I should have paid more attention to.

Joel's words echoed in Amber's head. Was he ever coming back?

As if in response, she could hear her grandmother's voice reply.

If he's fool enough to leave a girl like you and not come back, then he's too big a fool for you.

Maybe Nana was right.

CHAPTER FORTY-FOUR
JOEL

Joel decided to walk to the fight. The night was cool, and he had time to kill after not being able to nap for very long. The shelter had been noisy tonight, and he had too much on his mind to relax.

His father was dead. That thought spun around his brain, confusing him with the range of emotions it dislodged with each revolution. He was happy. Elated even, that he would never have to see Darryl's twisted scowl again. But there was also a deep rooted tension within him, bubbling beneath the surface. A dark rage whose source eluded him.

When Amber had told him about it, he hadn't been surprised, especially to know he'd been driving drunk. Darryl had done that all the time, and it was more amazing that it had taken this long for it to catch up with him. But the next thing that had gone through his head was that his death was too quick. Too easy. For all the pain and suffering he had inflicted on him and his mother, he would have preferred to hear about how Darryl had suffered a bit first.

Growing up, Joel had often fantasized about being the cause of that suffering. When he'd first started taking secret martial art training at school, the original goal had been to be able to defend himself and his mother. As time went on and he showed an aptitude for it, he started to imagine really laying into his father. He'd have dreams where he would pound the older man's face until it was barely recognizable and then wake up, his heart pounding. Not out of terror or fear, but excitement.

But he never acted on it. His mother would always defend Darryl, and then when she didn't stop the man from kicking Joel out, he realized that she probably still loved him in some sick and twisted way. He'd grown up trying to protect her from that monster, loving her and often placing himself in danger to protect her. When she sided with her husband in sending Joel out on his own with absolutely nothing, it had broken his heart and steeled his resolve that he was on his own in this world and could never really trust anyone else. Eventually, he came to appreciate that he owed his parents nothing, and he resolved to keep his relationships with others just as simple. If you didn't owe anything to anyone, then they had no power over you. He could leave whenever he wanted with nothing holding him back.

When it comes time to stick your neck out emotionally, you run away scared.

He let out a deep breath, trying to release some of the tension he was feeling as he thought about those words. Amber's interpretation of the way he lived his life was accurate. He had no problem with physical pain, but he really was trying to shelter himself from feeling anything emotionally. With physical pain you could figure out the cause and heal it. You could often fight back. Emotional pain stayed with you.

Just get out! He could still hear his mother's voice, as if she were right there beside him.

Amber was right in another way, too. He was living in the shadow of his past, unable to get on with his life. She was offering him a lifeline, trying to pull him in from an ocean of loneliness and he was throwing it back, telling her to let him drown.

Sounds of a crowd pulled his attention back and he realized he'd already arrived at the fight. The little parking lot behind the abandoned warehouse where they were fighting tonight was packed, and he saw Randy smile as soon as he saw Joel pushing his way through.

Randy introduced the fighters to the crowd a few minutes later as Joel pulled off his shirt. His opponent was a lean young black man who seemed like he couldn't be much older than 20, if that. He looked fresh, his body untouched and undamaged. To Joel, that meant that he was either very good or very new to this. Given his age, he guessed the latter.

His name was Tyrell, and according to Randy's introduction this was only his second fight but he had won the first one very quickly. When Randy announced Joel, he made particular mention of how he had lost his last fight, and hadn't fought in a couple of weeks but was trying to make his comeback.

Randy then told everyone that the fight would begin in 15 minutes and betting was now open. He walked around, collecting wagers as one of his employees helped by recording each one for later payouts.

Joel watched Tyrell. The young man was bouncing around, full of nervous energy. Whenever he caught Joel's eye, he would try to stare him down. Joel remembered acting similarly when he was just getting started.

"Joel?"

He turned and saw a thin bald man beckon him from the sidelines. He looked familiar but he couldn't quite place him. He still had a few minutes before the fight so he walked over.

"Glad to see you're healed up after the tournament at Golden Dragon," the man said. "I was looking forward to your fight with Carlos, a lot of people were disappointed that it didn't happen."

"No one more than me," Joel said. He must have recognized this guy from the crowd that night.

"You think you could have taken him?"

"I think he was lucky we didn't get to find out," Joel said. He still regretted not being able to slam his fists into the big

Hispanic's face a few times. Even if Joel lost the match in the end, that would have at least left him satisfied.

The bald man just nodded, his lips pursed as if imagining how the fight would have gone. "Well, good luck tonight."

Joel thanked him and returned to the center just as Randy was announcing that the match was about to begin. He wasn't thrilled about being recognized, but he figured it was unlikely anyone from Rock House would be here. Shawn spoke out against these types of fights enough that most of the fighters would stay clear of them. They'd have almost as much to lose by admitting they were here as Joel would.

The match started and Tyrell rushed Joel immediately, his nervous energy propelling him like a ball of fire to start the match. Joel sidestepped easily and swung his fist around to crash into the black man's midsection. He felt the bones of his hand pound against Tyrell's ribs with a satisfying thunk as adrenaline started to course through him.

Tyrell winced and spun around, throwing out a back hand as he spun that Joel easily blocked. He countered by lowering his body and delivering yet another shot to the same place. This time, Tyrell doubled over and stepped back. Joel let him, even though he knew he could have seized on the opportunity to leap forward and finish the match quickly. He was enjoying this too much, though. Both hits had sent a thrill of bloodlust up through his body, and he was beginning to imagine that Tyrell was really Darryl.

The other fighter recovered and moved forward, much slower this time, watching his opponent and keeping his fists near his face and his elbows by his ribs. The men circled, and Tyrell threw a few jabs. Joel danced away from them, thinking about how angry that made his father the first few times he had done the same to him.

Stop bouncing around like a pansy, boy, his father had said. *Come and fight me like a man.* His father hadn't seen the irony of that statement, as he threw his fists at the twelve-year-old.

Tyrell threw a wider punch this time, taking a shot at connecting with Joel's chin. This time, Joel stepped forward, letting the man's long arm swing around his head instead and now that he was close enough, Joel slammed the top of his head forward into the other man's nose. He heard a crunch just before he felt the spray of blood rain down across his shoulder. Tyrell fell back with a cry, his hands reaching up to grab his broken nose.

Joel wasted no more time. He turned on his heel and delivered a crushing side kick into Tyrell's torso, doubling the man over as he sank to his knees. His hands dropped to his stomach now as a puddle of blood began to instantly form below his down turned head.

Joel stood over him, waiting with his fist raised. As expected, Tyrell looked up to see what Joel was planning next. As soon as his head lifted, Joel's fisted came crashing down into it.

This is for you, Darryl.

The other man's limp body fell over onto his side and the crowd around Joel erupted in cheers. He hadn't even remembered they were there, he'd been so consumed with the hatred he had been unleashing. Was this how his father felt whenever he'd had too much to drink and wanted to flex his muscle against his family? The thought of that made Joel feel sick.

Randy ran up to Joel, raising one of his arms as the audience continued to hoot and holler at the brutality of the matchup. "You've won a lot of fans tonight," Randy yelled in his ear. "We need to schedule another fight as soon as possible to ride this momentum."

Joel nodded dully as he stared down at Tyrell's body. No one was making a move to see if he was okay, but he could tell he was breathing at least. His nose was a mess, and blood was still dripping down his cheek and onto the concrete below.

"Tonight was a big score," Randy was continuing. "I knew you'd win, that's why I tried to make the match sound like he was the favorite." He nodded at the black man who was now starting to stir. "Moved a lot of bets his way, which means more money for us. Close to $400 should be coming to you."

Joel nodded again. This was a means to an end, but it couldn't keep going on forever. He'd do what he had to do until he could figure something else out. For now, that money meant something important, and he wasn't going to waste the opportunity to make a change. It was time to stop drowning.

CHAPTER FORTY-FIVE
AMBER

Amber woke the next morning to a racing heart after hearing a sound coming from her living room. She leapt out of her bed in only her nightshirt and reached under her bed for the golf club she stored there.

Her door opened and she yanked the metal bar out and lifted it in front of her, ready to slam it down and run if needed.

"Whoa, easy there Tigress Woods, it's just me." Joel stood in her doorway with his hands up. He had a duffel bag slung over one muscular shoulder and was wearing a bright red T-shirt.

Amber dropped her arm down, the head of the club making a thud as it came to rest against the floor. "Oh, Joel. I wasn't sure you'd be back." She wanted to run into his arms, but she kept her voice cold as she struggled for control. She wasn't lying when she told him she was getting tired of this back and forth shit. She needed more stability in her life.

"I'm sorry," he said. "You were right. About everything. I have been afraid. Of this," he gestured to himself and then Amber. "Of committing. Of exposing myself to getting hurt again by someone I care about."

"I can't keep doing this," she said. Her heart was swelling in her chest, but she wasn't about to do this again without some assurance that he wasn't going to continue to leave every time they had an argument.

Joel stepped forward, the bag on his shoulder slipping off as he grabbed the handle and bent slightly to drop it to the ground. "I know," he said. "I've been thinking a lot about what you said and what you did."

Amber opened her mouth to protest, but she closed it again when Joel raised his hand and continued.

"I'm not blaming you anymore," he said. "I get that I can't expect to have a real relationship with someone if I'm not willing to let them in. I have nothing to hide anymore, Amber. Not from you, anyway. I kept my past a secret because I was ashamed of it. Not just of the way my parents treated me, but of whether I was going to turn out like them.

"I've been thinking lately about why I fight. I mean, I need to earn money and I don't have a lot of skills, and I'm good at it... but I've been wondering if there's something more? Like, maybe my father passed on some of his violence to me. Maybe it's in my blood. And I think I've been afraid that if you knew where I'd come from, or if you suspected that violence was more than just a job for me but was part of my DNA, then you wouldn't want to be with me. And I couldn't blame you for that."

"Oh, Joel," she said, letting out a deep and shuddering breath that she'd been holding while he spoke.

He shook his head again, not finished. "I just want you to know, Amber, that even if it is in my blood... even if there's something deep in my cells that drives me to keep fighting... I will never, ever, lay a finger on you. I will never hurt you. I'd kill myself before I'd do that. I won't become my father. I won't become a monster. I swear it."

Amber blinked as the image of Joel became distorted behind the tears that welled in her eyes. "I know you won't," she said softly.

"So anyway," Joel said, clearing his throat, "if you're still open to my moving in-"

Amber crossed the short distance between them and grabbed Joel hard by the front of the shirt and pulled him forward, her lips cutting him off in mid sentence.

He responded immediately by opening his mouth and taking control, his tongue pushing back at hers and asserting dominance. He moved his hard body closer so that they were touching and Amber could feel the heat coming off him in waves.

Joel's arms wrapped around her body, completely enveloping her as his hands caressed her back, massaging gently with his fingertips. His mouth slipped away from hers and continued along her face, pressing gentle kisses along her cheek and down the contours of her neck. Amber's breathing quickened and she put her own arms around his waist, pulling him closer and feeling his arousal pressing through his pants and against her belly button as she did.

"Joel," she moaned as his hands dropped lower down her back and found the edge of her night shirt, slipping underneath to grab her bare ass firmly. Lifting her up with his strong hands, he pulled her to him and she wrapped her legs around his waist as he spun and leaned forward. The two of them fell onto her bed with him on top, still clothed, between her spread legs. His hands were on either side of her, supporting his weight from pushing down on her completely.

As soon as they hit the mattress, Joel's mouth moved back against hers, kissing her with a renewed urgency. She responded, pulling him closer with her legs as his tongue probed deep into her mouth. She wanted more of him inside of her, though. Still kissing him, Amber slid her hands in between them and pulled violently on the button of his pants until it was undone. She yanked the zipper down and then hooked her thumbs into his waistband as she tried to work them down his hips without breaking contact with his lips.

Joel dropped one of his own hands down along her body and touched her calve, running along the smooth skin with his rough and calloused hands. A shiver ran up Amber's spine and she trembled as he moved it further up and onto her thigh.

His warm fingers continued their ascent, slipping under the thin cloth of Amber's nightshirt and past her belly until he had hold of one of her breasts, his thumb caressing her sensitive nipple. She gasped as soon as he made contact and ground her hips upward against the small amount of flesh she had been able to expose on him.

"Take them off," she whispered, pulling her mouth from his momentarily and then resuming where they had left off. No other explanation was necessary as Joel withdrew his hand from her shirt and wiggled his pants down. She felt his legs move as he used them to kick his clothes free until he was naked from the waist down.

Amber glided her hand down his hard body and wriggled it in between them as Joel shifted his weight to his supporting hand and lifted his body a bit to let her through. She grabbed him firmly, the hot and hard power that throbbed in her hand only serving to further feed her desire. "I need... this..." she said, squeezing him purposefully.

The fighter grunted in agreement, and she pulled him toward her entrance. He brought his hand back up and into her shirt, and just as she felt it grasp her breast again he thrust forward, merging their bodies as he filled her. She took a deep breath, bending her knees up along his abs to allow him to push even deeper.

His hips pressed hard against hers as they both took a second to get used to each other's bodies before he began to pull back. When he started to inch himself forward, Amber urged him along with her ankles, pulling his ass toward her. She wasn't interested in gentle and slow right now. She wanted hard and she wanted fast.

As if reading her mind, Joel's hips began to rock back and forth between her legs, going from slow and steady to a frenzied pounding within seconds. She closed her eyes, focusing on the pleasure that grew within her depths and then gasping as he added to it by biting the nape of her neck lightly as his index finger and thumb pinched her nipple.

"Fuck, Joel, keep going," she pleaded, moving the hand she had used to guide him up to her own swollen nub and rubbing along in time with his pounding.

Joel began to grunt with each thrust, and his speed increased, indicating that he was also very close to an explosive finish. Amber bit her lip as her legs pulled him ever deeper each time their bodies met. She felt him start to expand within her just as she reached her own peak. With a shuddering moan, he released, filling her with a hot fire that she could feel blasting deep inside of her. Her own body was quivering now as well, and she could feel herself undulating and squeezing against his hard flesh. She pulled him even closer, unwilling to let him pull away until they had both stopped trembling.

When he finally did, he rolled over to lie next to her, both of them wearing only their shirts, although hers was hiked up over her breasts which she was grateful for since it meant the heat of her body wouldn't be trapped around her.

"So, I also wanted to ask you something else," he said, after he had stopped panting.

"Anything," Amber turned her head to him and smiled.

"The other day, when we were fighting, you called me your boyfriend..."

Amber could feel her face get hot as she giggled nervously. "Yeah, sorry. That was a Freudian slip or something."

"No, I liked it. I mean... it's kind of high school, but I like what it means. I don't want anyone else, Amber. Just you."

She smiled at him and rolled up onto her elbows, bending down and kissing him on the lips again. When she pulled off, she lay her head down on his chest and closed her eyes, a big smile spread across her face.

Maybe he wasn't such a fool after all.

CHAPTER FORTY-SIX
JOEL

Later that day, Joel explained to Amber that the only way that living together was going to work for him was if he could contribute. To that end, he told her that he would split the rent and bills with her fifty-fifty. He felt bad, but in order to explain how he would manage his half, he made up a lie about Shawn giving him some work to do at the club that he could do after they closed at nights.

The lie served two purposes. For one, it explained his sudden influx of cash. But just as important, it also explained away how he would be coming home late some nights. He figured even if he only fought once a week, it would be more than enough to cover the expenses. Anything over that he could just save for emergencies. If he showed Amber too much cash, it would be suspicious anyway, since it was unlikely Shawn would be paying him very much for doing odd jobs after hours at the club.

For a few weeks, things went along perfectly. His training and conditioning at the gym were improving his technique and stamina, and he was winning all of his after-hours fights for Randy. Occasionally he'd come back with a noticeable bruise or black eye, but those were easily explained away. He would tell Amber that he got it during training, and he would tell each of the guys that he had got it the previous day from one of the other guys when they were sparring. No one asked questions. Injuries were part of the job.

"Why the big smile," Amber asked him one morning, about a month after he had moved in.

"Isn't rent due today?"

Amber squinted at her boyfriend with a little frown. "Yes... so again, why the big smile?"

Joel shrugged. "I don't know, I've never paid rent before. It feels kind of nice to be able to, I guess." He handed her an envelope filled with his half.

Amber threw her head back as she laughed. "I don't think I've ever met anyone who was happy to pay rent before." When she saw Joel's smile fade a bit, she walked up to him and cupped his cheeks in her hands, pulling his head down until their foreheads touched. "I know what you mean, though. I think it's sweet." She pressed her lips to his and gave him a hard kiss to emphasize her point.

"I got you something else," he said, pulling away from her and opening her closet door. He reached up to the top and stuck his hand between the extra blankets that were out of her reach, pulling out a rectangular black box. It was almost as big as a shoe box, but much thinner. He handed it to Amber as she gave him a questioning look.

"What is this?"

"Open it," he said.

Holding the box with one hand, Amber lifted off the lid with the other. When she saw what was inside, she inhaled sharply.

"You said you didn't have one," he said, reaching into the box. He pulled apart the ends and pushed his hands through her red hair to place it around her neck and then stepped back. Amber hadn't said anything, she was just staring down at the empty box in her hand.

"I think it fits," he said. "I don't think it comes in different sizes."

Amber finally lifted her head, and when she did there were tears streaming down her face. "I can't believe you remembered..." Her hands reached up and she touched the metal disc that hung around her belly, running her fingers around its edge.

Joel shrugged and reached up to wipe away the tears from her face. "Can't be a nurse without a stethoscope, right? Think of this as just the first step toward your dreams."

Amber leapt forward, tackling her boyfriend onto the bed behind him and kissing him, running her fingers through his blond hair, pulling his face close to hers and biting on his full lips. "You're amazing," she whispered.

* * *

Joel was almost late for his training session that morning after Amber had insisted on demonstrating her appreciation, over and over. He almost had to fight her off trying to get her to let him get ready to go.

He sped through his training, his mind on other things. As usual, he spent most of his time studying technique and working on his stamina, foregoing weights and strength training. He was more of a technical fighter and figured he would have time to build up more power behind his punches later. For now, he decided it was more important to be able to last long enough to go for the submissions he had been perfecting. In the past, many of his wins came from those submissions and he wanted to concentrate on his strengths. Chris argued that he needed to be more well rounded, as there were times where your opponent forced a boxing match no matter how much you wanted to wrestle. Joel could see the value in that, but he would have time to focus on that later.

He was fighting tonight, and it was a big one. His opponent was from out of state, but rumored to be unbeaten. He was on vacation and looking for some action while away from home. Randy had told Joel it would be a big payday because there were a lot of people that had heard about this guy and wanted to see him fight. He figured winning this one fight alone would probably net Joel over a grand. Maybe a lot more.

When he finished at Rock House at around six, he went through his normal routine. He headed to the shelter nearest to the fight for a nap, and then woke up in time to walk to the venue. This time it was inside of an abandoned factory. When he got there, the parking lot was full and he could hear the noise from the crowd even before he opened the front door.

Inside waiting for him was the biggest crowd he'd seen at one of these. Easily a couple hundred people, and he could see that Randy was already walking around with his assistants, taking bets. When he noticed Joel, he waved him over and they stepped away to talk privately.

"You ready for this one, kid?"

"Of course," Joel said.

"This guy is big," Randy said, motioning with his head.

Joel looked over to where he had indicated. Standing by the wall of the factory was a huge monster of a man. His arms were thick and corded with muscle, and his long legs reminded Joel of tree trunks. He had tattoo sleeves running up both arms and seemed to have virtually no neck that Joel could see. He went from broad muscular shoulders directly to a head that was topped with a closely cropped haircut that looked like it had been done at a military barber. Joel tried not to look disturbed by the size of the man and just nodded.

Randy laughed nervously. "Well, the bigger they are the harder they fall, right? That's what they say." He clapped Joel on the shoulder. "Good luck, kid. We start in five." Randy returned to the crowd to continue collecting bets.

He's big, but can he fight? Joel knew from experience that size didn't really mean anything if there wasn't enough technique to back it up. This guy was unbeaten, but who knows what the competition was like where he came from. Joel had been training with actual professionals. He'd been working a lot on his stamina and technique lately. Surely he had the advantage.

As big as this guy was, he'd have to lug all of that weight around. Probably tires him out pretty quickly.

"Joel, hey!"

His attention shifted to the familiar bald man that had recognized him from his tournament. He'd seen the man come to a few of his fights since then, and wasn't surprised to see him here again today.

"That's one big mother fucker," the man noted.

"So is Carlos," Joel responded. "But I'll still happily kick his ass if I ever get the chance."

The other man gave a slight nod, pursing his lips as if he was doubtful, but too polite to say it. Joel shrugged and turned away. He'd dealt with doubters all his life. He usually proved himself with his fists. He wondered whether he'd ever get the chance to do that with Carlos.

Walking back through the crowd, Joel pulled off his shirt as Randy started the introductions. The crowd cheered when he announced Joel. He imagined how much louder it would be if he ever made it to the big time, fighting in massive Las Vegas casinos or city stadiums.

Then Randy introduced his opponent who apparently went by the nickname the Executioner. The crowd roared even louder when they heard that. He wondered, not for the first time, whether he should have a nickname of his own.

The fight began and both men approached each other. As Joel suspected, the big man wasn't quick, and he started to strategize how to use that to his advantage. Each step the man took was an awkward forward shuffle that led with his right leg as he seemed to drag the rest of his bulk up behind it.

His opponent was standing in a traditional fighting stance, with his right arm raised near his face, squared off with his right knee, and his shoulder facing Joel. As they got closer, Joel noticed the tattoo that was plastered across his entire upper arm. It was a very detailed image of a muscular man with a black hood draped across his head and face. His hands held a sharpened axe that lay across his shoulder, dripping blood. The entire tattoo was black and white except for the blood, which was bright red. He wondered which came first, the nickname or the tattoo.

Joel decided to make his move, anticipating a slow response from the big man. With a burst of speed, he swung his leg up and slammed it into his opponent, right under the raised right arm and then pulled it away before the big man could respond. He connected solidly, but the Executioner barely even flinched. Instead, he took another step toward Joel. Joel moved a step back, trying to keep out of reach.

The crowd reacted with a roar when he had thrown his kick, but now they booed as he moved out of reach, thirsting for more action.

He leapt forward again, this time throwing two punches at the big man's mid section and then slipping away just as his meaty arms came down to try and grab for him. And again, although his punches were solid, the other man didn't seem to be affected by the attacks.

Again the man advanced, and as Joel stepped back he reached the edge of the crowd behind him. Usually the circle would move as the crowd kept a relatively equal distance between themselves and the fighters. Tonight, though, they weren't getting out of the way. Joel wasn't sure if it was because there were a lot more people here than usual, and maybe they just didn't know the etiquette, or if it was because they thought they could force more action by blocking his retreat. Whatever it was, he was trapped from moving back any further.

Before he could decide what to do, the other fighter attacked. He took another step forward to close the gap and then threw a roundhouse punch at Joel's head. It wasn't quick and Joel had plenty of time to raise his arm to deflect it, but the sheer power of the other man pushed right past his block and his fist connected with the side of his head, knocking him off balance.

He could hear the crowd around him roar as they finally stepped back, anxious to not become part of the action themselves. It was too late for Joel, though. He tried to stagger back out of the way, but the Executioner moved forward again before he'd completely recovered. Another fist drove into him, this time hitting him right in the face after once again pushing past his guard as if he were a white belt on his first day of class.

Joel felt his nose explode on impact, covering his mouth and chest in hot, wet blood. The power behind the bigger man's punches seemed impossible to him, each one like a wrecking ball. He'd been hit in the head plenty of times before, but never so hard.

As his opponent raised his fist again, Joel leapt forward, pushing past the pain and dizziness and thrusting himself inside of the big man's reach as he slammed his own fist into the side of his huge head.

The Executioner's chin moved to the right on impact but then snapped back, a humorless smile plastered across his face. He reached around Joel's neck and grabbed him in a iron-gripped head lock. Joel threw his knees and elbows at each exposed part of his captor's body, but each one may as well have been thrown against a brick wall.

Suddenly, he felt that massive fist crash into his face again, and then again. A pressure was forming around his head as it was squeezed, reminding him of when he'd try to pop a zit back in high school. His last thought was whether or not his head was going to explode in a similar manner as the room darkened around him.

CHAPTER FORTY-SEVEN
AMBER

"Oh my god, what the hell happened?" Amber cried out as Joel staggered through the door. She'd never seen him like this, not even after he'd lost the fight the night they'd met. His face was a mess. His nose looked crooked, and there was dried blood everywhere. His left eye was black and completely swollen shut.

He opened his mouth to say something but then began to cough into his hand. When he brought it away she saw the bright red shine of fresh blood on his palm.

"Shit, Joel, you're coughing up blood? You might have an internal injury, we need to go to the hospital!"

"No," he croaked. "It's just from my mouth." He opened his mouth to show her his left canine was missing, the gap still oozing blood.

Amber gasped at the sight, but a thrill of relief flooded through her as she realized it wasn't something more serious. She was still horrified at the sight of him. She reached forward and put her arm around him, leading him to the couch.

"I'm going to get some ice," she said after sitting him down. There was a welt on his forehead the size of a baby's fist. "What happened?"

She hurried to the kitchen, putting some ice in a paper towel and worrying about her boyfriend. The last time he'd been injured seriously he'd had a concussion that was left untreated for a while. If he was hurt badly this time as well, he'd never admit it.

Joel was laying down across the couch with his eyes closed when she returned. He still hadn't given her an answer. Her lips pressed tightly as she pressed the ice to his head. He opened his eyes in surprise at the sudden cold.

"You were fighting in alleyways again, weren't you?" she accused.

Joel closed his eyes again, but he mumbled a response.

"What?"

"I said it was an abandoned factory, actually."

Amber pressed down hard with the ice against his welt, causing him to gasp in sudden pain.

"You promised me you were done with that," she said.

"I know. I'm sorry."

"Why the hell would you do this again, Joel?"

He didn't respond for about a minute, and Amber wondered if he had fallen asleep or passed out. Then he took a deep breath and opened his eyes again. At least, she thought he was trying to open them both. The swollen one was too battered to tell.

"I wanted to live with you. I wanted this to work. But the only way I could convince myself to do it was if I could pay my way."

His voice was quiet and weak. Was it because he was tired and hurt or ashamed? She wasn't sure. "There's no job at Rock House, is there?"

Joel's head moved slightly before he winced. "No. I'm sorry, Amber."

She let out a long and shuddering breath. She was angry that he lied, and even more so that he put himself in danger again. But now wasn't the time to deal with that. "I know. Are you sure you don't want to go to the hospital? I think your nose is broken."

"It is," he said. "But no hospitals."

"Fine," she said. She removed the towel from his head and took the ice out, placing it on the table next to the couch. Then she gently wiped away the dried blood from around his nose and held the towel against his nostrils. "Blow."

The towel turned crimson as he did.

"How long ago did this happen?"

"I don't know, maybe 30 minutes? I took a cab back afterward."

It was cutting it close, but she could still help. She raised her palms and brought them together and then lowered them so that they were touching the top of his nose. "This is going to hurt," she said.

She pressed firmly as Joel exhaled in pain, bringing the bottom of her hands together under his nose. Then she pulled her palms down the sides of it, putting pressure until it looked to be roughly straight again.

The final step was inserting a finger into each nostril, aligning it from the inside as well. Picking up the towel, she instructed Joel to blow out again. More blood and pus came out.

"Where'd you learn that?" he asked when she was done and started to stuff tissue into his nostrils to help keep it set and absorb any more blood.

"The benefits of having a wannabe nurse as your girlfriend," she said, shrugging. "But you really should see a doctor. I don't know if it's going to stay straight."

Joel grunted. "I wouldn't be the first fighter with a crooked nose."

She shook her head at his stubbornness. "Well, you might as well sleep on the couch tonight, I don't think you're in any shape to clean up and I don't want you bleeding all over the bed." And she was still mad at him. "We can re-evaluate in the morning after we see how you look."

"Okay," he agreed. His eyes were already closed again. Amber stared at him for a few more moments before sighing and turning toward bed herself.

***

Joel's nose looked a bit more crooked in the morning than when she had left him, but it was still a lot better than when he had first come home.

"It's going to set that way if you don't go to a doctor," she said, standing behind his shirtless body as they examined him through the bathroom mirror. Now that they had washed away all of the blood, it was easier to evaluate his injuries.

The bump on his head had already receded a bit, so Amber wasn't that worried about that wound. His nose, although crooked, would be fine as well. But his eye was completely swollen shut and he couldn't even open it this morning. He had some other pretty angry looking bruises on his body, but they were less serious. When she had pressed along his rib cage, although he was tender, she could tell that nothing was broken.

She scoffed at him when he mentioned possibly still going to Rock House. "Are you kidding me? Are we looking in the same mirror?"

He shrugged and turned away, walking back into the living room and returning to the couch.

"I think I'm in trouble," he said.

Her heart sped up and she sat down next to him. "What do you mean?"

"Rock House has a policy of no outside fighting. Shawn basically said if I continued I would be kicked out."

Amber took a deep breath and closed her eyes as she let it out slowly. *Then why the hell didn't you stop?* She knew the answer, though. His twisted sense of obligation to not feel indebted to anyone. If he wanted to live here, he needed to help pay the bills. "You'll have to lie," she said.

"What am I going to say? It's pretty obvious this came from a fight."

"Okay, so tell him you got in a fight but it wasn't because you were competing or anything. Tell him it was a bar fight."

Joel raised his eyebrow.

"Shawn knows me, he knows I work at a bar. He knows you're a hot head. Tell him you came to the bar where I was working last night and saw some guy giving me a hard time. One thing led to another and you ended up like this."

"I think he'd probably question why I couldn't defend myself against a drunk," he argued.

"Fine, tell him it was a group of guys if that satisfies your macho need to look tough," she said. "Anyway, if he questions how beat up you look, just say 'You should see the other guys.'"

Joel laughed. "That might work."

"Tell him to call me if he doesn't believe you. I'll convince him."

Joel smiled and leaned forward, giving Amber a gentle kiss on the lips. "You're amazing," he said. "No matter how much I fuck up, you're always there to bail me out."

She kissed him back. "How about you stop fucking up for a little while?"

Joel kissed her again. "I'll try, Amber. I promise. I know living with me isn't simple."

"Sometimes I think getting in the ring with you might be easier," she teased.

Joel's look became serious as he pulled his head back a bit to look at her. His blue eyes seemed to draw her in as she waited for him to speak.

"I think I love you," he finally said.

Her heart was pounding in her chest. She hadn't been sure he would ever be able to tell her that. "I love you, too," she replied. "And I don't have to think about it."

He leaned forward and their lips met, and then he bent down and swept an arm under her knees, lifting her from the ground with a little wince as he carried her to the bedroom.

"Are you sure you're up for this?" she asked, giving him a little kiss on the earlobe as she held tightly around his neck. He was injured, but she still hoped he'd say yes.

Joel nodded and smiled at her as he lowered her onto the mattress and slid alongside of her. "Just be gentle with me."

She giggled and swung a leg over her waist, pulling herself on top of him as she looked at his battered face. It didn't matter what he looked like, she really did love him. "Fat chance of that." And then she lost herself on his lips.

CHAPTER FORTY-EIGHT
JOEL

Joel took a couple of days off to heal before heading back to Rock House, at Amber's insistence. When he returned, Shawn asked him to come into his office.

Joel was impressed when he stepped into the owner's private room for the first time. Plaques and framed magazine covers adorned the walls from when Shawn was still a competitor. There were trophies and medals on display as well, but he didn't have time to examine them as much as he would have liked.

"So a bar fight, eh?" Shawn sat down behind his desk and picked up a little blue stress ball, working it in his hand as he looked up at his young protégé.

Joel nodded, sticking to the story he had already gone over on the phone when he had called to tell his trainer that he wouldn't be in for a couple of days.

"Joel, I know I made myself clear the first night that you weren't supposed to continue your after-hours fighting, although obviously if this was really just a case of you defending your girlfriend, that's another situation altogether."

"If you'd like, you could call and talk to her. She should be home, she doesn't work today."

Shawn's gaze drilled into Joel, his bottom lip pulled down below his teeth before he finally put the ball down and exhaled heavily. "I have no doubt she'll tell me the same thing," he said. "Look, Joel, I don't know what happened for sure. Maybe your story is true, and maybe it isn't. And since I don't know for sure, I'm not going to do anything about it. But let me be clear. If anything like this happens again, you're out.

"I know shit goes down, but you're going to have to learn to walk away. If something comes up that makes you think you can't handle shit on your own, I want you to come to me first. Let's see if we can come to a solution together. I know you haven't had an easy time of it, which is why I gave you a shot here. I see potential in you. Don't fuck it up."

"I understand," Joel said.

"Now get out of here and go train. Lay off the sparring for a few days while that nose heals a bit more. You don't want it any more crooked than it already is."

As soon as Joel closed the office door he let out a long hard breath that he'd been holding. Shawn obviously didn't completely buy his bar fight story, but at least he was still training. He needed to make sure he didn't fuck up again. He may not have earned anything from his fight with the Executioner, losers never did, but he already had enough money from his previous fights to keep paying rent for a few more months. Until then he had time to figure something else out. Maybe he could ask Shawn if there really were any odd jobs around the gym that needed doing - turning his initial lie into a reality.

For now though, he needed to do as Shawn suggested and double down on his training. He needed to stop being distracted by other things.

He walked over to the free weight section. Most importantly, he needed to start working on his power, like Chris had suggested. He wouldn't let brute strength be his undoing again.

* * *

It was already past dinner when he left that night, one of the last ones to go home. As he walked through the parking lot toward the bus stop, he heard someone calling his name. It turned out to be the bald guy that he'd seen at his fights a couple of times.

"Hey Joel, how's the face?"

"It's healing," he said. "I hope that other guy's fists will be okay though."

The other man laughed. "At least you can joke about it."

Joel nodded. "What are you doing here? Looking to join a training camp?"

The other man cocked his head. "You don't remember me, do you? I didn't think you recognized me, but I wasn't sure. I looked a bit different, of course. Had a goatee."

"Have we met before?"

"Not officially. I was one of the fighters in the tournament at Golden Dragon. My name is Darien."

As soon as he said it, Joel remembered him. He'd fought against Carlos and gotten creamed. "Oh right, I remember now. Sorry I didn't recognize you before."

Darien shrugged. "No worries. Anyway, I still train at Golden Dragon. With Carlos."

"Oh," Joel said. "I guess you aren't one to hold a grudge then."

"A fight's a fight. Nothing personal. Carlos is damn good and he beat me. I figured if I'm going to train from someone, it should be someone like him."

Joel didn't say anything. He had his own feelings about the big Hispanic.

"You hear he was signed to a fight with Titan? It's going to be television in a few months."

Joel nodded. It was a big opportunity for a fighter. If you did well in one of these smaller televised events, it sometimes led to a bigger contract shortly after with a more well known organization.

"Anyway, he wants to talk to you. He asked me to find you. He told me you were training in the Rock camp now."

"What does he want?"

"You'll have to ask him yourself. I have a car here, we can go right now."

Despite his feelings about Carlos, Joel was intrigued as to what the other man could possibly want to talk to him about. As far as he knew, the enmity between the two of them went both ways. He nodded and followed Darien to his car, but his body felt tense. He would be ready for anything.

CHAPTER FORTY-NINE
AMBER

As much as Amber enjoyed being able to help nurse Joel back to health during the last couple of days, it wasn't how she wanted to spend the rest of her life. There just seemed to be some sort of self destructive streak in that man that she couldn't seem to figure out how to shut down.

She hated that he had lied to her, but she understood why he'd done it. Or at least, she understood why he felt that *he* had to do it, although she still didn't really understand why he felt that way in the first place. To understand that, she would really need to know more about his past.

The last time she had dug into his family life had ended up in a huge fight, but they'd gotten through that. During the last few days, Joel had actually started to open up a little bit about his childhood. Nothing major, but enough that Amber could see he was making an effort to let her in. Nevertheless, she was worried that it wasn't going to be fast enough. There was no telling when the next time would come that he'd self destruct.

After finding out about his father, she had hoped it would change things. One demon of his past was vanquished, but something else still hung over him. There was still a part of him that wouldn't give himself over to her completely. He still seemed to be waiting for the other shoe to drop. As if he was surprised any time he came home to find Amber still there, waiting happily to greet him. It broke her heart to imagine what could have caused such hurt in the man she was growing to love so much.

So although she knew the potential to completely backfire was high, she still felt like she needed to dig a little bit deeper. She needed to go somewhere that Joel may never forgive if he found out, but if what he'd said about his past was true, he probably would never find out anyway. He'd left all that behind, and it didn't seem like he was ever going to go look for it again.

She picked up the piece of paper that she had written the number on and picked up the phone. She held it in her hands for a few minutes before her shaking fingers started to dial.

"Hello?" came the voice on the other end.

"Is this Mrs. Slater," Amber asked.

"Yes. Who is this?"

"Do you have a son named Joel?"

There was a long pause on the other end of the phone. She was about to say something, thinking she may have been disconnected, when she finally heard the other woman answer quietly. "Yes. Is he...?"

"No, oh god no, he's fine," Amber said. She hadn't even thought about what a call like this from a stranger, out of the blue after so many years, might sound like to Joel's mother.

"I'm a friend of his. His girlfriend, actually. I was wondering if I could come and talk to you?"

CHAPTER FIFTY
JOEL

Darien drove them back to the club where he'd first met Carlos, the Golden Dragon Dojo. He had a bad taste in his mouth surrounding the place, still believing them to be a bunch of crooks after they had required him to pay $300 to join just so he could fight in the tournament. That was one membership he never planned to use.

Darien dropped him off at the door. "He's just inside, the door should be open. The club is officially closed right now, but Carlos has special after-hours privileges."

Joel watched as he drove off, wondering if coming here was such a good idea after all. He'd promised both Shawn and Amber that he would behave, and he couldn't afford to break that promise again. But if he was going to meet up with Carlos alone in an empty dojo? There was no telling how that would play out.

The sign on the door said closed, but when he gave it a yank found that it was unlocked, as promised. Inside he was surprised at how different the place looked than it had when he'd last been here. Of course, at that time it had been set up for a tournament, with bleachers and a ring. Those were all gone now, and instead the floor was covered with mats. There was some seating along the side of the room, but there were only fold up chairs. Unlike Rock House, there was no workout equipment in sight. It was a more typical Dojo than MMA training house, which made sense. The tournament he had fought in had been co-sponsored by Tiger Strike. That training camp had their own facility.

The main part of the Dojo was empty, but he heard laughing coming from one of the rooms at the back so he made his way across the mat. There were a few doors along the back wall which looked like they led to offices and change rooms. The men's room had a light on and the door was not closed all the way. The sounds were coming from in there.

"Hello?" he called through the opening. There was laughter coming from inside, both male and female voices. He wasn't sure anyone heard him so he said it again, louder.

"Come in," yelled the male voice. He recognized the accent as Carlos immediately.

Joel wasn't prepared for the sight before him as he stepped through the doorway and turned toward the source of the voices.

Carlos was sitting on a long bench that he'd pulled up next to the lockers and he was leaning on them. His long pony tail was still slicked back, but he was only wearing pants. What surprised Joel, though, was that he wasn't the only one shirtless. There were three women sitting with Joel, all of them only wearing bottoms.

The first girl, a brunette, was in jeans and on his lap. Carlos had his arm around her bare chest, covering only the nipples of her very large breasts.

There was another brunette on the bench leaning against them on their left side who was in a short black skirt. As she saw Joel enter she giggled and put her hand over her smaller breasts, covering both of them completely.

The third girl, a blond, was sitting on a second bench that had been pulled perpendicular to the first. She was facing the other three with her bare back toward Joel. She looked over her shoulder as he came in and smiled.

"Hey ese, it's been a while," Carlos said. He had a little smile on his face, but his attention was clearly split between Joel and the girl on his lap. His hands were moving around her chest as he spoke, and she brought her own hands up to grab his to keep them in place. There were two empty wine bottles on the floor, and double that many beer bottles. A half filled bottle was on the bench to Carlos' right.

"Carlos," Joel nodded. He still hadn't a clue what the man wanted, although he was fairly sure it wasn't to join him in an orgy.

"I hear you've been talking trash about me at one of those little underground fight clubs," he said. His fingers squeezed the girl on his lap and she let out a little yelp.

"I wouldn't say that," Joel said carefully.

"Darien tells me that you said I was lucky that we didn't get to fight. He said you wanted to kick my ass. What do you think girls? Do you think this little runt could kick my ass?"

The girls all giggled. The brunette on his lap shook her head.

"Maybe we should find out, eh ese? We could go right now, let the girls judge the winner?"

"You're drunk," Joel said. "It would be easier than normal and then you'd have an excuse about why you lost."

Carlos' eyes darkened and his hand flattened against the bench as he launched himself to his feet, throwing the brunette off of his lap, her big breasts bouncing freely for a moment before she covered them up and scampered off to sit on the other side of the bench. The other brunette slid over to sit next to her.

"Even drunk I could take you," he roared, spit flying from his mouth.

"I'm not here to fight you, Carlos," Joel said. "Is that all you wanted to talk about?"

"Darien told me you got your ass handed to you the other night. Your pretty face doesn't look so pretty anymore," he laughed, his earlier anger already dissipated. "I wonder, how did you explain that to Mr. Rock? From what I hear, he has a zero tolerance policy for after-hours fighting. Maybe I should call him and ask him why he made an exception for you?"

This time it was Joel who could feel the temperature in his neck and face start to rise. "Is that your plan to get rid of me? Sabotage my training? You didn't strike me as the type to be scared of a fight."

"Scared? Of you?" Carlos threw his head back in an exaggerated laugh. "Like I said, if you want to fight right now, let's do this." The big Hispanic started to open and close his fists by his sides, as if loosening them up.

It took every ounce of willpower that Joel possessed not to leap forward and knock Carlos in the teeth. "And like I said, I'm not here to fight right now. But I think it's a great idea. It's time we got in the ring."

"Name the time and place," Carlos said. "Do you think your master will even let you off your leash?"

That was the problem. Shawn Rock would be furious if he fought Carlos outside of an official fight, and he'd probably kick him out immediately. But perhaps there was a way he could swing it.

"You let me worry about Rock House. You worry about Tiger Strike and Golden Dragon."

Carlos laughed again. "Neither of them have any rules about what I do outside of training hours," he said. Joel's eyes quickly shifted around the room to the three women he was partying with in the Dojo, the blond winking at him as he met her gaze. *Clearly*.

"Fine," Joel said, turning on his heel and exiting the way he'd come. "I'll set it up. It's finally time we do this." He left before Carlos could say another word. If he hurried, he could make it back to the club before Shawn left.

CHAPTER FIFTY-ONE
AMBER

Amber almost drove through a red light, the honking horn of a passing pickup the only thing pulling her mind back to driving. She was already late, although it wasn't as if there was a set time she needed to be at the club. There were only a few times a year that Rock House allowed spectators in to watch training, ostensibly to entice new sign ups, but on those days it was open the entire day. Still, she had told Joel she would be there in the morning, and it was already almost lunch.

She hadn't expected Linda Slater to call her and want to finally talk, but after a month of only getting bits and pieces out of the woman, she had been reluctant to turn her away. When Amber met her that first time at a coffee shop in Joel's old neighborhood, his mother had been wary. It had been a long time since she had heard anything about her son and although she seemed eager to hear about his life, which seemed strange after what Joel had said about her, she was also very close lipped about the past. Amber figured that after what the family had been through, she had been reluctant to talk to a stranger about it.

But Amber had been relentless, going to visit or calling Linda on the phone at least once or twice a week, always when Joel was training, and slowly she could tell that the older woman was becoming more and more comfortable with her. She certainly never turned Amber away, and asked a lot of questions about Joel. She was very interested in what had happened to him that night that he'd left, how he'd gotten by over the years, and what his feelings were about his mother. Amber didn't think there was a reason to soften the blow in regards to that last issue given how they'd treated Joel, and yet Linda seemed to take the news of his hatred very hard. It was perplexing.

But as much information as she asked of Amber, she was reluctant to give anything back. That is, until this morning when she called Amber's cell phone out of the blue. She said that it was because Joel's birthday was coming up, and that was always a particularly hard time for her. She didn't want to go for another year without seeing him again. Amber told her that meeting him wasn't a good idea, and that was when she decided to open up.

The conversation spun through her head, distracting her from everything else. She needed to just focus on getting to the club and what, if anything, to tell Joel. She hadn't agreed with Linda about seeing him just yet, although the woman was quite adamant. Amber wasn't sure how much longer she could put her off, but she definitely didn't think right before his big fight this weekend was the best time.

She arrived at the club and pulled into the busy parking lot, stopping in the shadow of the towering Rock House sign. She was impressed with the building, it was a lot bigger than she had pictured it.

"Hello," said a friendly looking young woman who was standing at the door to greet her as she walked in. "Are you a friend of someone at the club?" The good looking blond had her hair tied back in a pony tail and wore a tight fitting tank top that showed off her very muscular arms. Amber wondered whether she trained there. Joel had never mentioned any women at the club.

"Um, yes, hi. I'm with Joel. Joel Slater. I'm his girlfriend." She hated that she felt the need to add that last part in, but the blond intimidated her and she wasn't happy that Joel hadn't mentioned that there were girls here. He did spent a *lot* of time at this club, after all.

"Great. I think he's over on the mats, doing some sparring. You can just follow behind the ropes to the far end of the facility," she said with a smile, pointing. "Just stay on this side of the ropes so as not to disturb the training, and try to keep any noise to a minimum. If you have any questions, feel free to ask me or anyone on your side of the ropes wearing a Rock House shirt or uniform."

"Okay, thanks," Amber said, returning the smile and heading toward the fighters. The girl seemed very friendly, and Amber felt guilty about her earlier twinge of jealousy.

She had to press through a number of spectators, mainly men, to get to the other end of the club. The size of the place was impressive, and there were fighters everywhere. Some were lifting weights or kicking a heavy bag, others were stretching, and there were even some fighting within the full size rings that she had noticed when she first came in.

The majority, however, were sparring on the mats and all of them wearing similar outfits and headgear. It was impossible to even determine which one was Joel.

"Amber!"

She turned to see Shawn Rock approaching , walking just inside the rope to keep out of the way of the fights.

"Hi Shawn," she said, smiling broadly. She'd always have a soft spot for Shawn Rock after what he'd done for Joel.

"My wife Sarah mentioned you'd just arrived," he said. "Does Joel know you're here yet?"

His wife? Amber let out a little relieved breath. "No, I don't even know which one he is?"

Shawn laughed and turned to scan the fighters behind him. It took him a moment, but then he pointed. "Over there. He's fighting with Blake. He's definitely come a long way in the last couple of months."

"Do you think he's... I mean, the fight this weekend..."

Shawn nodded, still looking out at the men on the floor. "I think he's ready to fight Carlos. Certainly a lot more so than he would have been during that first tournament. And even then it would have been a pretty interesting match to watch.

"You know, when he first approached me with the idea of setting up a match between Rock House and Golden Dragon, I was hesitant. I knew what his initial motivations were. But then he explained how we could turn it into a big event, a rivalry between the two training camps that would drive business to both... well, I'm glad I listened to him." Shawn gestured at all the people standing around.

"Last time we had an open house, we didn't have half these numbers. I think anticipation about this weekend has been very good for the club. I think Joel has a good head for promotion. Anyway, if you'll excuse me." Shawn gave her a quick smile as he returned the way he'd come.

Amber nodded back and then turned to watch Joel spar with the bigger man he was up against. She wasn't so keen on the idea of him matching up with Carlos either when she had first heard the idea. The difference was, she hadn't come around to it much more since then. Carlos seemed like a mean son of a bitch, and every time Joel had to fight anyone she felt sick with tension and worry. The one saving grace was that this time it wasn't a tournament. Joel would only fight once, as would everyone else who fought that night. Less fights meant less chance of injury. *At least I hope that's what it means.*

She saw his opponent, Blake, hit Joel with a right hook and then pounce, taking her boyfriend to the ground. The two rolled around a bit, but then Joel somehow ended up on top with the other man's arm between his legs as he twisted. Blake tapped firmly on Joel's back and then Joel let go. The two men parted and stood up, loosening their helmets.

As their heads became visible she saw them talking to each other. Blake didn't have a very happy look on his face, but she did see him give what looked like a begrudging nod to Joel as he turned and walked away. Joel turned as well, and she waved to get his attention. He waved back and started to make his way toward her.

Despite the fear she felt any time he stepped up to another opponent, Amber couldn't deny the other feeling she had. There was definitely something thrilling in seeing her man take down someone else, especially when his opponent was bigger and stronger looking. She almost felt ashamed, but she had to admit that it turned her on just a little bit. If he did end up pounding the hell out of that asshole Carlos, he might have another wrestling match to look forward to that night.

Joel looked at her funny as he approached, so she did her best to stifle the silly grin she felt starting to grow across her face.

CHAPTER FIFTY-TWO
JOEL

Joel knew that Marcus Flores was just playing a mind game when he agreed to this bout only under the condition that they do it at his club again. In a way it made sense, though. Joel and Carlos would get a rematch to the finale that never was at Golden Dragon Dojos, where the original had taken place. There was already a built in audience for that, and it would have been silly to disregard that fact.

But he also knew that Carlos was Marcus' man, and letting him fight on his own turf while pulling Joel back into the place where he'd ended up so injured was also a way to try to fuck with his head. Carlos was the prize fighter of the Tiger Strike team which, Joel hadn't realized at the time, was also run by Marcus. Effectively Tiger Strike and Golden Dragons were the same entity, the latter just existing separately to be able to also reap the financial benefits of also training non MMA-hopefuls.

He sat in the bleachers with Amber, waiting for the place to fill up and everyone else to arrive. The setup was the same as before with the ring in the middle and the black curtain separating off the fighters from the crowd. The only difference this time was that in the back there was a second black curtain separating Tiger Strike from Rock House. It was a good idea, as there was a lot of bad blood between the two groups, even aside from Joel and Carlos. In fact, many of the fights on the card tonight had been long simmering grudge matches between members of the opposing camps.

"Nervous?" Amber asked him. Her hand was resting on his thigh and she gave it a little squeeze as she spoke.

He shrugged. "Not really." It wasn't nerves as much as anticipation. He just wanted his fists to connect with Carlos' face a few times.

They sat in silence, watching the crowd filter in and get seated until Marcus and Shawn made their way into the center of the ring and began to talk. The two of them announced the line up, and gave plugs to their training camps at the same time, anxious to wring as much publicity out of the event as possible. Joel had no problem with that, he knew that was the primary reason the whole thing was happening in the first place. That was how he'd sold Shawn on the idea, after all.

The judges were then announced. Both Shawn and Marcus both discussed the three officials, with each man being able to veto a suggestion if they thought there was a potential for bias. They ended up agreeing on David Page, a DJ from a local sports radio station; Amin Zofu, a newspaper sports columnist; and Fiona Gelles, a former ring girl from many televised MMA events. Fiona was a gorgeous blond that Joel thought looked familiar when he saw her. He'd obviously paid more attention to the ring girls when he'd watched pay per view fights than he'd ever admit to Amber, who he noticed was giving him a sidelong glance as Fiona was being announced.

"Well, I better get back there," he said, giving Amber a quick kiss on the lips.

"Good luck," she said, reaching out and grabbing his hand. She seemed reluctant to let it go as he pulled away to head to the curtains. He couldn't blame her, after what had happened last time. He'd ended that night in a pretty bad state, but he had no intention of ending things similarly tonight. If anyone left on a stretcher, it would be Carlos.

Joel had never felt more prepared for a fight. He'd been training harder this past month than ever before, working on adding power as well as technique to his game.

He pushed past the curtains and joined his fellow Rock House team behind the curtain. Blake looked up as he entered and gave him a little nod, walking toward him. "You ready for tonight, Slater?"

Joel nodded at the tattooed team lead.

"Yeah, I think you might be after all. Watch out though. I've seen Carlos fight a few times. Don't get cocky. He's a tough son of a bitch." He nodded again and walked off to talk with Kingston. Coming from Blake, that was just about the highest praise he could expect. The man had softened considerably toward Joel since they'd first met.

"Did I hear that right, did Blockhead actually say you might be ready to fight Carlos?" Joel turned to see Chris smiling at him as the man raised his fist and bumped it to Joel's. "I think you might have injured him permanently the last time you put him in a headlock."

Joel lifted a lip in a half smile. "Blake's okay," he said.

"Man, I gotta go and see if pigs are flying, I'll be right back," Chris said, laughing as he clapped Joel on the back and walked away to mingle with the other fighters.

The announcer began to talk, and then he heard him start to call out the names of the first two fighters. Rorie McMahon was up, and he soon disappeared through the curtain. *Let the games begin.*

CHAPTER FIFTY-THREE
AMBER

She didn't know what was worse, waiting for Joel's match to come or actually hearing his name and knowing it was about to begin. She'd watched each fight with a growing tension, as Joel's turn grew closer. Now that it was only a few minutes away, the anticipation had formed a knot in her stomach that she knew wouldn't be gone until the night was done and Joel was safely in her arms at home, in bed. He had a way of working on all of the little knots in her body that actually created an increase in tension at first, but always left her much more relaxed by the end.

She was smiling to herself as she thought about some of those releases when a commotion at the end of the bleachers distracted her. The crowd to her right were standing up as someone was pushing their way past.

She stood to let the person by as well, but when she came into view Amber gasped and fell back down into her seat. What the hell was Linda Slater doing here?

When Joel's mother saw her, she gave her a thin smile and then squeezed herself in next to Amber. Her long, dirty blond hair was pulled back and tied into a loose pony tail, leaving her blue eyes free to look apologetically at her son's girlfriend.

"What are you *doing* here?" Amber whispered, as soon as Linda was seated. There was no one listening or who would even care within earshot, but she felt like she had to keep her voice down or somehow Joel would come rushing out from the back swinging his arms wildly or something. She had to get rid of his mother before he saw her.

"Well, you weren't letting me talk to Joel and I told you, I need to. It's been long enough. I won't wait any longer."

The apologetic look had faded now, replaced by defiance as she was forced to justify herself.

"How did you even know where I was?"

"I'm not stupid," Linda said. "Although Joel might have expressed differently to you, god knows he has every right to believing it. You've mentioned enough things about him over the last month that I was able to put the pieces together. You said he had a big fight this weekend, and this was the only one I could find around town anyway." She shrugged.

"You have to leave, Linda. I'm serious, if Joel sees you-"

"I'm not leaving now that I know my boy is here," she cut her off. "I haven't seen him in years, and after the way he left I didn't think I'd ever see him again. You don't know what this last month has been like, knowing he was out there and finding out what he really thinks about me. I mean, I knew what he must think, but it's different once you hear it's true."

"Linda, if Joel-"

"There ain't nothing you can say that will change my mind, Amber," she argued. "I'm sorry if you think Joel will be mad at you for finding me, but what's done is done. Anyway, there's no way he'll ever be as mad at you as he is at me. And I just can't live with that anymore. I want to talk to him. I want a chance to explain."

"And you'll get that chance, I promise. Just not now. This fight is important and if he sees you, it will distract him for sure. It could throw him off his game. He's fighting someone very big and strong and even without a distraction I'm worried about his safety."

"And you think telling me that he might be in danger is going to make me want to leave?" she asked. "Anyway, I've seen my Joel in a lot of fights and trust me, he's learned to handle himself."

"Mrs. Slater, with all due respect, this fight is a lot different than with... than the fights you've seen Joel in."

"All the same," she said, turning her head to look out at the empty ring. "If Joel is going to be fighting tonight, I'm going to be here for him when it's done, win or lose. That's not something I've always been able to do for him, but I can do it this time."

Amber sighed, closing her eyes and terrified at what Joel was going to do when he saw his mother. *This isn't going to end well for any of us.*

CHAPTER FIFTY-FOUR
JOEL

"You ready for this?" Shawn Rock was standing in front of Joel, his eyes gleaming.

"I am," he replied. "I have been for a long time."

"Cool, cool. Listen, I just heard something interesting. Apparently there are a couple of scouts out there in the audience tonight. Carlos has a TV deal with Titan and they sent some execs out to watch his fight."

"So what does that mean?"

Shawn got a sly little smile. "Well, look, I'm just saying that if Carlos was to get his ass handed to him out there, I wonder how eager they would be to put him on television." He laughed. "Then again, you never know. Every fight has to have a loser. But it would still take some of the smug look off of that fucker's face, anyway."

The announcer called Joel's name and Shawn patted him on the back. "Anyway, go out there and do your best. We both know you're good enough for this fight. Time to show Carlos."

Joel nodded and parted the curtains as he strode through, ready and as confident as he thought possible. He felt strong and ready to put on a good show, anxious to finally be getting into the ring against his nemesis. He quickly scanned the crowd for Amber, hoping to give her a confident smile that would reassure her that everything was going to be okay.

He spotted her, but instead of looking at him she was talking to a woman sitting next to her. He couldn't see the woman's face as she was turned toward Amber, but something seemed vaguely familiar about her. Then Amber caught his eye and she turned to him, giving him a little wave but with a weird expression.

As he was about to wave back, the other woman turned to face him as well and he almost tripped over his own feet. He stumbled, but then regained his balance by grabbing onto the ring just as he got to it.

What the fuck is my mother doing here?

The blood sped through his veins causing his face and body to get hot as his heart rate sped up. He was clenching his fists and staring into the crowd, barely aware that the referee was calling his name. He shook his head, snapping himself back to attention and hoisted himself up and under the rope.

He was barely aware of Carlos being introduced next, his eyes never leaving the two women sitting side by side, watching him not 20 feet away. *What the fuck is she doing here, and how did she know to find Amber?* As he gazed at his girlfriend with a raised eyebrow, she mouthed an apology and he could feel his blood boiling even more. *Sorry? That means she had a hand in this somehow.*

The announcer was giving the crowd the details of the match, though they hadn't changed for any of the fights that night. Three rounds of five minutes each with one minute of rest in between. He was taken by the arm and he walked duly along to the center of the ring, only then realizing that Carlos was there and ready to fight. They touched gloves and the bell sounded, snapping him to attention.

Carlos wore his full Golden Dragon gi, and Joel was fighting shirtless and in loose pants, as usual. The big man's hair was slicked back in his standard pony tail and he was glaring at Joel with eyes the color of midnight. Before he'd even had time to raise his hands after touching gloves, Carlos' fist shot forward, catching Joel on the chin. He had side stepped just a little too late to avoid the blow, but it was enough that the attack hadn't hit him full force, although it did snap his head to the side quickly and daze him. His hands went up in defense instinctively, blocking the follow up blows that Carlos tried to deliver.

The men circled each other, Joel struggling to remain focused on the fight instead of what was going on in the crowd. *Why would Amber invite his mother to this fight? What the hell was she thinking?*

He threw a few quick jabs at Carlos but he easily blocked them, returning a punch and then a spinning round house kick that Joel ducked. Normally he would have seized the opening Carlos had provided with the kick and attacked before he dropped his leg, but his mind was too unfocused and he thought of it a split second too late.

The men again resumed their defensive postures. So far, there had been very little action, and the crowd was starting to yell. Joel saw the big match clock counting down with only a couple of minutes left in the round. As soon as it was over, he would get to the bottom of why the hell his mother was here and get Amber away from the bitch, even though he knew that Amber had to be the reason she was here in the first place. *How else would she have tracked me down?*

Carlos threw another roundhouse kick and it caught Joel in the ribs before he'd had a chance to block it, again letting his thoughts slow his reaction. However, as his arm was already on its way down for the block, he ended up grabbing the other man by the calf even as he winced in pain from the kick.

With his leg trapped, Carlos threw a punch toward Joel's head but he was ready, blocking it with his free hand. He took a step forward, pushing Carlos and causing him to hop backward on his one grounded leg and bend forward for balance. As he did so, Joel lifted his knee and grabbed Carlos by the head with his hand at the same time, driving his leg up and crashing it into Carlos' nose.

He felt the heat of fresh blood explode against his pants as Carlos let out a roar, pushing back with a burst of adrenaline and freeing himself from Joel. But the damage was done, and his nose was a steady stream of blood that left crimson raindrops and streaks across the top of his white uniform.

Joel went to advance again, but Carlos held him off until the bell rang, signalling the end of the first round.

Chris was waiting in Joel's corner as agreed, giving him a quick drink and talking quickly. "Good ending, Joel, that one rocked the fuck out of him. I think his nose is broken." His friend's missing tooth was the only dark spot in his smile.

Joel smiled back, knowing how Carlos felt right now. His own nose had fully healed since his fight with the Executioner, but it would never be as straight as it once was. He used that as a reminder not to ever let himself get caught unprepared again. As he thought about it now, he decided to use it as a reminder to not let himself get distracted, either. Both problems could be equally dangerous. *I'll deal with my mother and Amber when this is done. Now it's time to focus.*

The bell rang and he headed back toward Carlos. His corner had stopped the bleeding in his nose for the moment, but Joel knew it would be tender and ready to open up again at the slightest touch. Which meant he had a target.

This time, the two men came out swinging. Joel threw punches aimed at hitting Carlos in the face again, and Carlos blocked and continued to deliver an assault of his own. Both men were caught multiple times, and half way through the round there was blood drawn on both fighters and the crowd was going wild. Joel had a cut over his eye that was dripping down his face, blurring his vision, while Carlos' nose had opened up again and his own eye was swollen.

Despite the conditioning Joel had been doing to build his stamina, he was starting to feel the heaviness in his arms and legs as he continued to exert so much energy in his attacks. Carlos was breathing heavily as well, and with less than two minutes left in the round the men found themselves in a clinch, holding each other around the shoulders and using the time to rest while also making slight adjustments to their stance in an effort to find some advantage against the other fighter.

With less than a minute to go, Carlos made a quick move, grabbing Joel around the neck and pulling him as he stepped outside his legs, yanking him down and landing on top in a side mount. He began to drive his elbow down onto Joel but only got a few hits in before the bell sounded to end round two.

"Okay, let's look at that eye." Rock House had a cut man for Joel to use in his corner, and he applied pressure and a quick acting coagulate to stop the bleeding while Chris spoke to Joel.

"The way I figure it, you had round one and round two was a toss-up, but may go his way because of that last throw. I think you had it until then, though, so it's hard to say. But assume you need to win this last one. Of course, a knock out or submission would be better..."

Joel nodded, figuring the match the same way and he stood up just as the bell sounded to start their final round. He doubted he'd be able to knock Carlos out, but a submission wasn't out of the question. But a win was a win, and he'd take a decision from the judges if it came down to that. He just needed to give them a reason to vote his way.

As soon as they met in the center, Carlos threw a punch that Joel caught with his wrist; he then leapt in the air, spinning his legs up over his head as he pulled on the limb in an attempt at a flying arm bar. Carlos came crashing down with him and Joel almost had him locked in, but the Hispanic was able to wrench his arm free at the last moment before he could apply pressure.

As Carlos tried to roll off, Joel grabbed his leg, locking it within his own and grabbing the ankle as he worked on a knee bar submission. Carlos rolled to get out, Joel rolling with him and continuing to apply pressure. Carlos' leg was bent at what Joel knew was a painful angle, but the fighter refused to give up, continuing to work on freeing his leg. He was able to turn enough to reduce the pressure, so Joel switched tactics again, grabbing the other man's foot in a heel hook, toe hold combo.

Carlos grabbed Joel's own leg, trying to apply an ankle hold of his own and forcing Joel to release his own hold to defend against his own foot snapping under the intense pressure of Carlos' submission attempt.

He was able to pull himself free, managing to continue his assault on Carlos. His submissions weren't finishing his opponent off, but at least they were keeping his opponent on the defense instead of the offense, which meant that points should be flowing mostly in Joel's direction. He attempted an arm bar, and even a rear naked choke, both of which were defended by Carlos. Carlos, in turn, was only able to hit Joel a couple more times with elbows to his face as the two men struggled on the ground. The hits weren't hard, but he did manage to open up the cut above Joel's eye again.

It wasn't long before new stains were appearing on Carlos' gi, adding fresh patterns to the stained fabric. Joel wouldn't let the injury stop him, though, as he continued his relentless ground assault on his opponent. By the time the bell rang to end their match, he knew he had done enough to win the round.

CHAPTER FIFTY-FIVE
AMBER

As soon as the bell sounded, Amber leapt to her feet along with the roaring crowd. The finish had been an exciting mix of grappling and wrestling which gave the round an exciting contrast to the pounding of the previous one, but that wasn't why she had stood up. Joel was bleeding, and she wanted to get over to see if he was okay.

The match had been a close one, but from the murmuring of the crowd around her, Joel sounded like he'd actually pulled it off. In the ring, he was surrounded by fighters from Rock House, some of them lifting his arm victoriously, all of them with smiles on their faces and patting each other on the back. Shawn Rock was right in the middle of it, his smile biggest of all. She couldn't even see Joel's face as everyone crowded him.

On the other side of the ring, Carlos looked in even worse shape than Joel, but his friends were also holding his arm up. To Amber's eye, they didn't look quite as confident. She pushed her way past the cheering audience, making her way to the ring. It would be a couple of minutes before the official decision was read, and she just wanted to see Joel's face and tell him how proud she was of him.

Grabbing the bottom rope, she hoisted herself up so that she was on the outside of the mat, looking over the top. Through the crowd, she saw Joel. His face had been wiped clean of fresh blood and someone had taped up the cut over his eye so that it was no longer dripping down into him. He saw her and immediately started to make his way over, his face a mask compared to the joy around him.

The other fighters saw where he was headed so stepped back to give him privacy with his girlfriend as they continued to congratulate each other and await the final result.

"What the fuck is she doing here," Joel said as soon as he was within earshot. He was glaring down behind Amber.

She turned to see Linda Slater standing below. *Damn. It's bad enough that she came at all, why the hell didn't she stay in her seat until I could explain things?*

"Joel, I can explain-"

"Joel, honey, my beautiful strong boy!" Linda was calling out from the floor, and there were tears coming down her face.

"Are you fucking kidding me?" Joel hissed at Amber, his eyes bright blue flames.

Amber shook her head, "I think you need to-".

She was cut off by the announcer. "Ladies and gentlemen, the judges have come to a decision!" The other fighters crowded around Joel again, lifting his arm and guiding him to the center of the ring where Carlos already stood with his teammates. The referee took the arms of both fighters.

"After three rounds, the judges have scored as follows. Judge David Page sees the fight as 48 to 47 for Alvarez." The crowd became louder with a number of boos coming through the noise.

"Your second Judge, Amin Zofu, sees the fight 48 to 47, Slater." This time, the crowd went wild, clearly agreeing with Zofu.

"Your third and final judge, Fiona Gelles, scores the fight 48 to 47 for the winner by split decision, Carlos Alvarez!" The crowd went crazy, with people yelling and booing. Inside the ring, chaos erupted as well. Rock House fighters looked angry and began to shout at the announcer, the ref and down at the judges tables. A couple of them began arguing with members of the Tiger Strike camp. Both Shawn Rock and Marcus Flores had to step in and stop what looked to be imminent fights.

Joel looked stunned as well, not seeming to listen to a couple of men that were standing next to him. A fighter with blond hair, streaked with red dye put his arm around Joel's shoulder and was shaking his head.

"What happened?" Amber heard Linda call out from below. "Joel lost?"

Amber looked down at her and nodded.

CHAPTER FIFTY-SIX
JOEL

"This is bullshit, what a crock of shit!" said Chris, his arm around Joel as he spoke into his ear to be heard over the booing of the crowd.

"What a corrupt bunch of assholes. Figures this would happen here. Shawn should have pushed for an independent venue!" he continued.

Joel was stunned at the decision, but his mind was focused on other things. He cast a sidelong glance at Amber. She was looking down at the floor below the ring, talking to his mother. His mother. He wondered again what the hell she was doing here. Did she think this match was going to win Joel some big money and she could somehow cash in now that her husband was dead? Joke was on her if that was the case, even if he had won the cash prize was only a few hundred bucks as a token gesture from the two training camps. Not that he would have given her a penny anyway.

"I'm sorry, Joel. That's completely an ass backwards decision. You deserved that win." Joel looked up to see Blake standing in front of him.

"Thanks," Joel mumbled. It must have really been unfair if Blake was even on his side.

The sounds of the crowd were starting to die down as the angry mob took their feelings out into the street now that the event was over.

Off to the side, he could see Shawn and Marcus arguing.

"They must have fixed it somehow," Chris was saying. "Bought off the judges."

At the mention of the judges, Joel glanced over at the table. Zofu had already left, but Fiona and David were still there talking. From his angle, he could see David staring at Fiona's chest through her top. Shaking off Chris' arm, Joel walked over to the side of the ring and looked down at them. Aware of being watched, they both returned his gaze. When David saw it was him, he turned quickly away. Fiona just smiled and winked.

It hit him like a fresh punch to the nose, he knew exactly where he'd seen her before, and it wasn't from TV. Fiona had been one of the girls who had been sitting topless with Carlos the night they agreed to this fight. She gave him one last half smile, as if she knew he recognized her, and then she took David's hand, leading him away toward the front door.

Joel closed his eyes as he took a deep breath. It was odd, but the loss didn't even bother him now that he knew it was fixed. The match meant nothing, really. He glanced over at the crooked and battered face of Carlos who was talking to another fighter. *I got what I wanted out of it.*

"Joel!" he turned to see Shawn Rock approaching. "Joel, I'm sorry about all of this. I don't know what happened with the judging, but something was clearly not on the up and up. I spoke to Marcus, I don't think he had anything to do with it but I can't be sure. But in my books, you won that fight hands down."

"Thanks Shawn," he said.

Shawn cocked his head toward one side of the ring. "There are a couple of people who want to talk to you when you have a minute."

Joel sighed. All he wanted to do right then was talk to Amber and find out what the hell his mother was doing here and then go home. He was still angry that she brought her at all, and he would definitely be having another talk with her about privacy and boundaries, but at the moment he was so overwhelmed with everything else that was going on that he didn't even want to think about that conversation.

He looked over at two men standing at the edge of the ring, talking to some of the fighters. They were middle aged, and wearing jeans and loose fitting shirts. Likely fans that wanted to tell him what a great fight he'd had, and that they thought he should have won. He really didn't want to hear that again, but since Shawn was asking he couldn't say no. Maybe they were friends of his.

"Just give me a few minutes, okay? Let me go and get cleaned up and then I'll come back out."

Shawn nodded and patted him on the shoulder. Joel walked back to Amber and slipped between the ropes. He jumped down and then helped her follow. His mother stood by, staring at him with a big smile on her face, as if the past had never happened and they were finally being reunited after years of being kept apart by something other than her own betrayal.

He glared at her, satisfied only when he saw her smile falter against his withering gaze.

"Joel," she said, reaching forward to try and take his hand, but he pulled it away.

"What the fuck are you doing here?" he said.

"Joel," she said again, this time keeping her hands to herself but wringing them nervously in front of her. "I can't believe you're here. I'd almost given up hope of ever seeing you again. I was afraid you were..."

"Dead? You were afraid I was, or hoping?"

She shook her head violently. "No, never!"

"Really? So casting me out with just the clothes on my back - to you that was what, good parenting? You thought that was the best way to get me to survive and thrive?"

She shook her head again. "No, no, Joel - your father, he wanted you out-".

"And so did you, Linda," he said, refusing to call her anything other than her given name and actually holding his tongue back from calling her bitch in front of Amber. "I clearly remember you screaming for me to get out. It's your voice I hear when I sleep at night! Not Darryl's!" He bit his tongue. He hadn't meant to admit that. He didn't want her to know what an affect she still had on his life. He didn't want to give her that satisfaction.

"Oh, Joel," she said, taking another step forward with her hands raised as if to cradle his head. He stepped back again, glaring at her.

"Why are you here? I have nothing to give you. And even if I had, I wouldn't."

"I don't want anything, baby. I just wanted to see you... Joel, please listen to me."

He felt Amber's hand snake out and grab his, giving it a little squeeze as if pleading with him to do as his mother asked. He held his tongue, giving his grudging acceptance through silence.

"Joel, that night... your father and I had a terrible fight. He told me that he wanted you to leave, and I told him no. But..." she was quiet for a moment, her eyes were filled with tears but Joel refused to feel anything. He just stared at her, waiting for her to go on.

"He had a gun, Joel. He was pissed off that you had learned to fight. To stand up to him. To protect me. He was fed up with it, and he said you were going to stop. One way or another. I don't know if he was going to do it, but he was drunk, and I was scared."

He looked over at Amber and her eyes, too, were filled with tears. She looked back at him but said nothing. She simply stared into his eyes.

"I didn't want you to leave," his mother continued. "But I was afraid that if you stayed he would do something. Maybe not that night, but at some point. You couldn't stay. So I did and said those things because that was the only way I could think of to keep you safe. I thought that if you just left that night and then came back, he might use that as justification to kill you and claim he thought you were an intruder. Or that you were coming back to kill him first. I don't know." There was another pause, and then she whispered one more time. "He had a gun."

And all of a sudden, Joel's world view shifted so violently he felt himself sway.

CHAPTER FIFTY-SEVEN
AMBER

Amber tightened her grip on Joel's hand as she felt him lean toward her, but he caught himself and straightened up. She was watching his eyes as his mother spoke, catching the precise moment that the words hit home.

"Joel, I'm so sorry," his mother said. This time, when she stepped forward, he didn't back away. She put her arms around him and squeezed, Amber stepping away to give them room. Joel stood there like a statue at first, and then he drew a deep shuddering breath as he slowly raised his arms and hugged her back. His eyes closed quickly, but not quick enough for Amber to miss the tears starting to form. She wiped her own eyes with the back of her hands.

"I thought I would never see you again. When your father died, I tried to find you but I didn't know how. I even put an obituary in the paper for that son of a bitch, thinking maybe you'd see it and come to the funeral... even if it was just to spit on him..." she trailed off with a huge wracking sob. "Oh my Joel baby, I'm so sorry!"

Joel's eyes were still closed, but Amber could see his grip around his mother tighten. He was never a man of very many words, but this time she didn't think any were needed. Joel's mother was still talking, but her words had fallen to whispers in his ear as he just nodded silently. She felt like she should give them a few minutes of privacy, so she turned back to the ring.

Shawn Rock was walking over, and he tilted his head to indicate she should come up, waiting until she had joined him inside before he spoke.

"There are some people who need to talk to Joel," he said.

"Is he... okay?" He glanced down to where the fighter was still holding his mother with a perplexed look on his face. He clearly knew Joel as well as anyone, so watching him hold someone so tenderly was obviously confusing to him.

Amber nodded. "He just needs a few minutes."

"Well, I think he's going to want to talk to these guys. Tell him they're from Titan." Shawn looked around. The ring was mostly empty now, except for the two men he'd referred to, and even the floor was starting to clear as most of the audience and fighters had already exited.

"Okay, let me get him."

She walked to the edge of the ring and looked over. Joel and his mother were no longer hugging, but were still talking quietly. She hated to interrupt, but she knew that Joel had all the time in the world now to get to know his mother again.

"Joel?"

He looked up at her, his eyes no longer misty.

"Can you come up for a minute?"

Joel told his mother he'd be right back and swung himself up into the ring again.

"These men over here want to talk to you."

Shawn Rock was over talking to the two of them when they approached.

"Hi Joel," said Shawn. "I want you to meet Nathan Zimmer and Umberto Bari. They work for Titan."

Both men were tall and slightly overweight, but all smiles as they reached forward and shook Joel's hand. "Great fight," said Nathan.

"Terrible decision," Umberto added. He had a slight Italian accent.

"You may or may not be aware that we've signed Carlos to fight with us," Nathan said.

Joel nodded. "I'd heard." His voice was flat as he said that, causing Nathan to laugh.

"You're not impressed? Well, we stand by that decision. Carlos is a good fighter."

"But maybe you're a bit better, yes?" Umberto added.

Joel shrugged, but allowed himself a little smile.

"Listen," said Nathan, "we want to sign you as well. Same deal that we gave to Carlos. Standard three fight contract, guaranteed to be at least on the televised undercard."

Amber's eyes rolled over to Joel and she saw his mouth open in shock. He didn't say anything, but luckily Shawn took over.

"Gentlemen, that is a very generous offer. I'll tell you what, why don't you leave us your card and we'll let Joel have a couple of days to think it over. We can call you from my office in a couple of days. Does that sound good?"

Both men nodded. "If you decide to sign with us, Umberto here will discuss the terms with you. He's also our sponsorship contact, and he can help set you up with the right sponsors for you who can help pay for the things you need while you train."

Shawn nodded and clapped Joel on the back, bringing some life back into the stunned fighter. "Um, thank you," he said, reaching forward to shake their hands again. They handed him a business card and then stepped out of the ring, leaving the three of them alone.

Amber's heart was fluttering in her chest, and she could only imagine how Joel must feel.

"You'll need a manager," Shawn said. "I can recommend someone if you'd like."

Joel nodded.

Shawn laughed. "You look like you're in shock. I think you need to take the night and let this all settle in. This is great news, Joel. You're going places. I knew it the first time I saw you. I hope you'll continue to train with us. Same deal as before. I know a big up and comer when I see one, and I know before long it'll be great for the club to have your name associated with us."

He clapped Joel on the shoulder one more time and said good night to the two of them.

Amber turned to Joel and leaned forward, giving him a soft kiss on the lips. His eyes seemed to focus again, oceans of blue that she would be happy to drown in.

"Come on," she said, grabbing his hand. "Let's go tell your mom the news."

CHAPTER FIFTY-EIGHT
JOEL

The last few days had been a whirlwind of activity for Joel, and he was happy to lay in bed on Sunday with Amber, her bare leg draped over his waist and the sweaty sheets cast onto the floor. Their breathing was just beginning to settle back down, but knowing Amber she'd probably be back on top of him giving him another work out at any minute. As enjoyable as that thought was, he wanted to talk to her first.

"I haven't had a chance to tell you everything that happened yesterday with Shawn," he said. He'd met with his trainer and Louis Gagnon, the manager who he had introduced to Joel a couple of days ago. Joel had asked the man to represent him, and together the three of them called Nathan and Umberto to go over the details of the contract they were offering. He'd only really told Amber that he signed, but then they went out to dinner with his mother and got home late. The morning had been taken up with other, more pressing activities and his stomach was growling for breakfast already. But he was anxious to tell her about what he'd decided.

Amber kissed his shoulder blade where her head rested, her red hair tickling his chin as she moved. Her hand slid down along his body to trace the contours of his abdominals. He knew from experience he wouldn't be able to concentrate for very much longer.

"So like I said, we signed with Titan for three fights to begin with. Depending on how things go, they may opt to add additional fights, but I'd be paid more for those and I have the option to say no."

"Why would you?" she said, her fingertips still lightly gliding up and down his stomach, but inching lower with each pass.

"I probably wouldn't, I don't know. Point is it would be up to me." That was important to him, at least. "Anyway, the pay for those fights is only a couple grand each, but there is a bonus that doubles that if I win."

"Which you will," she said. Her hand slid below his belly button and her leg moved lower so that it only covered his thigh now, exposing the rest of him to the warm air of the room and, more importantly, her exploring hands.

"Hopefully. They said my first fight will likely be against Carlos."

"Hmph," she said, her fingers pausing for a split second before continuing their descent.

"Anyway, the money from those will be nice, but the bigger payday comes from sponsorships. Umberto already mentioned a couple who are interested in signing me. Louis is going over the details. Usually that money is used to pay for a fighter's training."

"I thought you were going to continue at Rock House?"

"I am."

"Well that's great then! You'll get some savings together. Maybe we can finally move some place with better air conditioning."

"Maybe," he said. "But I was actually wondering if you thought you could handle the heat for a little bit longer," he said.

"Oh, sure. I guess so."

"It's not so bad at nights anyway, it's really only annoying during the day."

Her hand had stopped completely now. "Well, I know you're training during the day but I'm usually at home until I leave for work in the late afternoon. But yeah, I mean... we can stay here." He could hear the disappointment in her voice.

"About that," he continued, trying to keep the smile off of his face and from his voice. "I was thinking maybe you should change your schedule."

This time she lifted her head to look at him, annoyance forming creases in her brow. "You don't make money as a bartender during the day," she said. "It's just not practical. I thought you understood that."

"I do," he said. His smile leaked onto his face and it seemed to annoy her even more.

"So why would you suggest changing my schedule if you know I wouldn't make any tips?"

Joel put his arm over the side of the bed and reached under the mattress, pulling out a brochure. He sat up on his own arm, making a space between them and dropped it down onto the bed.

"What's this?"

"I think you aren't going to have time to bartend anymore," he said.

Amber picked up the pamphlet, but her furrowed brow remained. "Huh? Why are you giving me this? This is for a nursing college."

"I know," he said. "Sign up starts next week. Shawn is going to advance me the first semester's tuition and I can pay him back after my first fight and I get paid."

"I don't understand." Amber was shaking her head, but her eyes were glued to the papers in front of her.

"Amber, I don't need the money. I've never had any, and I can go without for a while longer without missing it. This apartment is cheap, and from what I'm going to get between the fights and the sponsorships, even if I don't win, I can afford to pay for this place and your tuition."

"Joel, I don't-"

"Shhh," he said, putting his hands over her mouth to stop her from protesting. Her lips were soft and once she closed her mouth he let his fingers trail across her cheek and then glide through her long red hair.

"Please don't argue about this, Amber. I want to do this for you. After everything you've done for me... shit, everything good that's happened to me in the last couple months has been directly because of you. I would never have any of this if it wasn't for you. I wouldn't have ever spoken to my mother again. Never heard her side of the story..."

His hands traced along the nape of her neck. "I would have gone my whole life believing that my mother thought I was a piece of shit, and I would have continued to hate her until I died. I would have continued to believe that there was no one out there who could love me, that I wasn't worthy of it... I would never have realized that I could love someone as well. That not everyone is out to just take. Some people give.

"You've given me my dreams. The ones I've held in my mind for years, but also ones I never even dared to have when I slept. I can finally repay some of that. You have to let me. I want to give you your dreams."

Amber looked up at him, her eyes misted over in tears and she leaned forward. "You already have," she whispered, pressing her lips against his. It was all the answer he needed.

COMING SOON
FROM AUBREY ST. CLAIR

SILVER AND CHROME

After Evelyn Silver walks in on her boyfriend/boss on the desk with his secretary, she ends both her relationship and her job. She is fine with the idea of being alone for a while and has no intention of getting involved with another billionaire megalomaniac. Always seeming to attract the wrong sort of man, Evelyn vows to take a break from dating for a while. So when her eye is drawn to Bash, a rough but handsome looking motorcycle club leader during a night out, she is determined not to get involved.

Unfortunately, when her ex begins to spread lies around town about her and her job performance, Evelyn's prospects of getting another job start to look bleak. The only option available brings her right back in front of the powerful biker as she stumbles onto the secret of a dangerous dual life that he leads. As his carefully constructed world starts to come crumbling down, the two of them are forced to trust and work with each other in order to try to save whatever they can.

But Bash must decide what parts of his life are worth saving, and what he's willing to give up in order to secure the one thing that's always eluded him. Love.

Printed in Great Britain
by Amazon.co.uk, Ltd.,
Marston Gate.